"In Artificial Intelligence, the closer we get to the human brain, the more chaotic and subversive the observed system becomes, as if it knows what we are after."

Dr. Deborah Rumford, *The Rumford Rogues*

The Rumford Rogues

Scenes from Consumer Life

By Colin Bennett

www.headpress.com

contents

one

Unintelligent Design

1. A Flatland Journey

MY NAME is George Mensche. I am a journalist working for *The Brentford Sceptic*, based at the Fountain Leisure Centre, Brentford.

You must excuse me. I am still somewhat mentally breathless after an exhausting trip to Manchester by rail. There I was supposed to do some research for my weekly column "Beacons of Britain." Some might think that a short one-day trip to Manchester from Brentford would not be particularly exhausting. But being born of the very oldest Highland aristocracy (I am a genuine Donald of the first waters), it takes me a bit of time to recover from a visit to what Dervorgilla my mother used to call "the plains." Anywhere south of Glencoe was an infernal region to my mother's mind, and inhabited by what she referred to as "the Flatlanders," the word *English* being *verboten* in my family circle. The word *Scottish* was banned also, this being regarded as an emblem of the lowland upstarts and the Caledonian *nouveau riche*.

To my great relief, the Intercity Express sped me back through flatness to my temporary refuge in time called London. This early May evening of the last years of the first decade of the twenty-first century happened also to be my "fortieth year to heaven," to use a phrase of Dylan Thomas.

Since I cannot eat Flatland food, I made the most of a packet of *Benson's Highland Cattle-Chews*, marked "fit for human consumption," and settled down in my second-class carriage to read Rabelais' *Gargantua and Pantagruel*. But something about the darkening Midlands scenery, flat as a dead Flatland film, destroyed my concentration. I took De Quincey's *Reminiscences* from my case, but I put that down in turn.

No matter what I did on this particular journey, each moment of experience transformed into elements of my early life. Train journeys are now old in the cultural tooth. They lead back into Time Past quicker than cars or ships. The past, I suppose, is always asking questions. Following such a transcendental path, we go back to those mysteries as yet unsolved, and those dramas of the deep past still developing.

But before I continue the tale of my return journey to London, let me introduce myself properly.

My name in what media folk call *real time* is Seeckt, and I am technically speaking a "von," but somewhere along a line of countless personal disasters, I acquired the name *Mensche*. One sarcastic Flatland ne'er-do-well from *The Ape and Parcel* (my local watering hole), guessed correctly that this was probably because of my brave cavalier attitude to a life consisting of one embarrassing personal catastrophe after another.

First, a confession. For my sins, I happen to be a direct descendant of King Duncan (1033–39), via the Tenth Duke of Hamilton (1767–1852). My father, the late Albrecht von Seeckt, connects me also to highest Prussian nobility and several historical figures. These include Hans von Seeckt (1866–1936), the German General who recreated the *Reichswehr* after World War I, later to become the *Wehrmacht* under Hitler.

Albrecht was a mercenary soldier, killed in a knife-fight in Brussels when I was very young. I vaguely remember him as an aquiline-nosed Prussian who unfortunately had Nazi sympathies. This was the reason for a troubled separation from my mother.

I hasten to add that as an *ancien royal*, I have no connection with that gang of Norman and German *Mafiosi* who occupy the Flatland throne, if indeed it can be called that.

It comes as no surprise to most people when I confess that I am not a reporter proper. Being in receipt of Social Security, pressure from the beloved authorities forced me to accept a part-time unpaid temporary "Work Experience" assignment with *The Brentford Sceptic*. I was told by a woebegone social worker that this scheme is part of a European Rehabilitation and Regeneration Scheme for High Born Unfortunates. Whilst such charity was welcome, the work involved was not. As could be expected, my old royal blood makes me marvellously useless. I have however a talent for limitless speculation of a somewhat abstract kind. Of course this does not make me the ideal person to interview the manager of *Knacker's Yard Brush Factory* in Manchester, which was the reason for travelling to that place on this day.

I strongly suspect that my journey to Manchester was a kind of apprentice joke rigged by the *management* (if it can be so called) of *The Brentford Sceptic*. Suspecting a trick, I did not try all that hard to find the wretched place.

I plotted my revenge in a Manchester supermart surrounded by nodding penguins who gave out McDonalds vouchers if questions about television soap characters were answered correctly. Inspired, I wrote a short piece on the Flatland mind. I conceived this as being made up of advertisements, game shows and commercial breaks rather than being a function of corpuscles and atoms (whatever they are). As usual, this will not please my editor Bill Price, a most practical ex-bricklayer from the northernmost Flatlands. Being born with such a lineage, I have great difficulty with the common or garden logic of the lower-case world. This is not appreciated by Price, who talks about DIY, media stars, and refers to television programmes in general conversation, a modern curse if ever there was.

However, more of this dolt later.

Since I could hardly carry around such wild genealogical baggage as was mine own, I used the name *Seekt* for a time, but I got letters from old ex-concentration camp prisoners promising that both my head and testicles would be obligingly separated from my body at the earliest and most convenient opportunity. I accepted therefore the lowly name *Mensche* as a matter of convenience. This name saved me from receiving fan mail from eighty-year-old Russian belly dancers, and monarchist mad-men still seeking all kinds of revenge after hundreds of years. The name protected me also from hippy trippers who supposed I was an original Celtic Lord, learned about Hobbits and fairies in the glen.

Watching the cities and villages of the Flatlands pass by, I remember my mother saying that the only things the people of such places talked about were their medical operations and soap episodes. She added that they spent the rest of the time having continuous rows about painting their coal cellars and wallpapering their bathrooms. This, said she, was to pass the time of the boring day and "prevent them all going mad in the Flatlands."

Though she inherited a great fortune, and indeed owned two castles, my mother still went out of a night and poached rabbits for a tradition-al stewpot. They tasted much better if caught illegally, she said, and she could well afford the countless fines and threats from magistrates and farmers, most of whom still doffed their caps at my mother's superior social status. This was my first lesson regarding the connection between imagination and what most unfortunates call the "concrete world." Al-ready to me the connection was messy, vague, governed by obscurities of tradition and belief.

I amused my mother one day with my threat that I would stew a purchased rabbit at the side of a poached one in a separate pot and see if they had a different taste. I did not carry out the test, but in any case this was my first and last scientific thought before I gave myself over entirely to my mother's contra-scientific opinions at a very early age. After she had downed a dram of *Glenn Grant* on a Saturday night, she said that the Flatlanders were "low" because they were geographically lower, so to speak.

Thus did I become profoundly addicted to metaphor. To me, it was always a far superior way of reasoning to fact. I associated fact with works managers with a row of pens in their top pockets, all (almost without exception) from the lower middle-class workshops and labora-tories, where they did unspeakable things with rabbits instead of eating them.

I was born with a very best Highland accent. Although it was quite incomprehensible to Flatlanders, my early mastery of late mediaeval Gaelic and *Erse* idiom was a great source of pride to my mother. My voice was equally astonishing. When only one foot high, I sounded like a First Lord of the Admiralty launching a *Dreadnought* battleship, circa 1905.

As I grew up, it became apparent that one of my personal characteristics had to be kept as a family secret, locked in the west wing as it were, like some mad son in the old novels. The "fact" (as the Flatlanders say) was that early on, brain was detected within my skull. People have no idea what this means to an aristocrat. It means that somewhere along the DNA net there has been hanky panky when the lights were out and nobody looking. It is the equivalent to buying a thoroughbred kitten with a pedigree as long as your arm and finding it developing the herring-tail of a moggie. Whispers were that such a thing could only come from the Hunnish von Seeckt family, since everyone for hundreds of years on the Gaelic side took a great pride in their inability to write their name or knock in the crudest of nails.

As such a secret moggie, I developed a habit of thinking deeply about esoteric matters, which was most disturbing to my defiantly non-cerebral mother. Fortunately, to her great relief, my thoughts and ideas were such that they had absolutely no practicality. In other words, they were no good to man nor beast. My mother, quite relieved, confessed to a concerned relative that she had feared at one time that I might finish up as a solicitor in London or (worse) Edinburgh or some such place. By the way, it was only once that I heard that dread word "Glasgow" at an uncle's funeral. He, who shall be nameless for his sins, lived in (whisper, please!) *Glasgow* in something called a *flat* — another word only heard in my mother's household on one occasion, when coming across an article on prostitution, my mother asked our Cook what was meant by the word *flat* in this context. Cook's explanation that the Flatlanders of the plains lived in flattened layers on top of one another caused my mother quickly to give up the ghost, as she had little technical concentration. She disappeared quickly into the vast interior of the manse, with the comment that this was what she expected of the two-dimensional folk of the plains.

I first knew I was going to have a lot of trouble in life when I declared to certain parties very early on that all I wanted to do was sit in a chair by a warm fire and read Gibbon, Josephus, and the great circumnavigations of the globe in their chronological order. As a three year old, I found I could not go out and get books and research material without causing great alarm in the neighbourhood.

My habit of wearing a tasselled *fez* and reading ancient Hebrew out loud caused an unfortunate family incident remembered by the local village forever and a day. A visiting dowager leaned forward over the precisely set tea table and asked my mother in rather confidential tones whether she had ever visited the Middle East at any time. Promptly, my mother stormed off into an inscrutable interior. The dowager tried in vain to get the butler to convey her most profound apologies. All the fellow did was to dedicate his entire lunch break to spreading the tale throughout the village. The result was that on quite a few occasions I got the greeting *shalom* from assorted serfs, mainly in grocery and provisions. I replied in ancient Latin and Hebrew, which rather put them in their place.

As soon as I could stand upright, I found that the body must be kept at a certain temperature, and protein must be injected at regular intervals, rather as if a human being were some kind of permanent invalid through being disastrously designed. I soon learned that promissory notes must be obtained, responsibilities honoured, and proper dignities kept. In addition I found that social behaviour must be monitored constantly, this meaning that those peculiar things called relationships must be developed, particularly with regard to the supply of property, commodities, and above all, vanities, reputations and inspirations.

Luckily, I managed to avoid that chattering draper's shop of wasteful bough-plumage called normal healthy human intercourse. At an age when most are still trying to distinguish between poo, pop, and pudding, I had already written a book on twentieth-century military history, and a tome on early Greek science. I used photocopies of original sources from the four corners of the British Museum and the Bodleian brought by servants, obligingly provided by my mother.

By the age of six I had also translated from the original Latin half of *Jewish Wars* by Josephus, correcting many mistakes made by Milner and Whiston.

By the age of fifteen, it could have been predicted that it was not going to be very long before my further interest in Hakluyt and Holinshead, Froissart and Tacitus, was subjected to fortunately not-very-determined attempts at what Flatlanders called *normalisation*. This phrase, thought I, was limited to Communists and social workers, both of whom already at that early age brought me to salivation as quickly as flapping crow to cat.

A problem came in the form of an old colonel of the Seaforths, with a great deal of influence over my mother. He had some Lowland blood, and he commenced a process of what he called re-education designed deliberately to reduce me to one of those woolly-minded pieces of universal scrap called a well-balanced human being. The result of these pathetic attempts was that at the age of sixteen, for three hours each Saturday morning, I was turned into something between a wheelbarrow, a crane, and a car-jack at *Deeton's Universal Stores*. This was in order (to use that peculiar phrase of not-too-bright Flatland normals) to "take me out of myself." The local medical impostor (constantly being consulted about me), had also recommended such a thing. Not because he had the usual pseudo-scientific views, but probably out of spite after being warned by yours truly that a mean blade would be put across his Chinese eyes if his "qualified" hand ever came near my cherubic hindquarters.

This early experience of forced labour involved packing crystallised fruit with croaking tin-frog gifts. I made sure my first acquaintance with such normalisation-socialisation-industrialisation and my first commitment to political correctness was screwing Mr. Deeton's comely Flatland wife Alice so heartily and so often that she took to religion (fortunately pagan). What with that, and the chopped mouse heads I inserted in Alice's celebrated *Quince Jam Preserve*, both the Universal Stores and the Devil did well out of the relationship.

As soon as I was conscious of it, I was very disappointed with my body. I saw it as a disastrous lump of rather messy suet, whose intakes and outputs must have been designed by the divine equivalent to an unsuccessful pig farmer. Where God's sublime touch was when the body's troublesome pipes and drains were plotted, I do not know. A pathetic twelve volt power supply is not nearly sufficient for the average body weight. Vision, traction and physical strength are poor, and bits fall off each of us as regularly as parts off a Friday Sierra (as they used to say in a pre-robotic world now as long gone as Nineveh and Tyre). These constant failures alone must make the human body one of the most comically disastrous bio-machine cock-ups in creation.

Such thoughts and observations did not fit well with the Colonel's attempts to give me that contradiction in terms called a scientific education. There was Trade in the Colonel, something of the Flatlands geography and spirit both.

Naturally, I threw away the shiny rationalist tracts containing all their tragi-comic promises of advancement, improvement and side-splitting "solutions" to the human predicament. I refused also to read books illustrating how the world "worked" in ten easy stages.

Fortunately for me, my mother cast aside the said Colonel (who was hopelessly in love with her). His drinking, gambling, and his outrageous modern enthusiasms saw him off to a bedsit in Perth.

Thereafter, my mother proceeded to rid me forever of contamination by the affectations of such Weights and Measures folk. I was not sorry to see the Colonel go from our lives. He was a Lowlander converted to a Flatlander by that kind of socio-political osmosis which had almost effaced the Scottish aristocracy from the face of the Earth. Whilst certainly he was above the level of a typical Flatlander proper, his mechanistic opinions did not make for a good entrance to the very best of natural-born Highland society.

My mother said for example that the lack of geographic contrast in places such as the aforesaid Manchester did something to the mind, somehow reducing it to two dimensions, and the television finished off what was left. "You have to be careful in cities of the plains," she said, "People bump into you because they can't see all of you at once, so to speak. They are flat screen-folk, who live in the two-dimensionality of the plains," quoth she. "They become obsessed with it. That's why they are always ill in body and mind. The other dimensions push and pull to get in, but they can't, and this causes conflicts which result in illness and disorientation."

To my growing mind, this connection between illness and spatial conceptions was quite superior to accounts of cells and atoms, molecules and particles of the Flatland folk, who consumed such things as readily as they feasted on the well-advertised *Skegness TV Reality Rashers*. My mother had other interesting opinions, such as her belief that the blessed Flatlanders (the word "British" was never used in our household where straw still lined an earthen kitchen floor), were the only people in the world who sat down and watched television. From the Philippines to Greenland, she added, they all had better things to do.

My mother's account of the origins of Christianity also impressed me during childhood. I remember her saying that a breaking of wind by Eve in the Garden of Eden was the cause of the First Couple's being cast out by God. This was the true form of the Serpent of Eden, said she. Sin, as such, had nothing to do with sex — sex came much later, and had much less theological significance than "God's mistake," as she called flatulence.

I remember agitated conversations about whether it was Adam or whether it was Eve who first released their personal gas upon the virgin Earth.

This elemental connection of the Holy to the Gut was, to me, much more significant than fairy stories about the origin of Sin. This version of the myth gave me great consolation during periods of doubt and uncertainty in life, of which I have had more than most.

As I explained to many a young maid who happened momentarily to lose control of her pipes, this was something to be proud of.

This, said I to many a blushing female possibility, was nothing more than an archetypal echo within her psyche of that original blast of sublime chords heard upon the Creation of the First Days. According to my mother's account of the legend, the sound accompanied the progress of the Star of Bethlehem. Though, said she, it had been long edited out of history by conspiratorial scholars of the newly emerging lower middle classes. It was, said my mother, Samson's last act before bringing the Temple down; such a thing also blew down the walls of Jericho and consumed mightily the topless towers of Ilium, though, as my mother explained, this was not mentioned by Homer for political reasons.

Many of my private tutors, unimpressed by my illustration of the connection between theology, history, and the smoking emanations of the noisy bowel, fled to more fragrant pastures.

I was equally enlightened concerning concepts scientific. A teacher, in order to illustrate the motion of the pendulum, told me to imagine a man sitting on a swing. Whereupon I proceeded to ask the name of the man. Quite astonished, the teacher told me that the man did not have a name. Nonsense said I, how can this man on the swing not have a name? Was he some kind of political prisoner?

Think of the man as a mere weight, the teacher told me. I said that to think of a man as such was absolutely insulting. It reduced the man (whoever he was) to almost nothing. I wanted to know more about this man sitting on the swing. I wanted to see a home and family, new shoes and ancient cats; I wanted images of atmosphere, character, ambition, not Weights and Measures ideas from the Flatland trading classes.

Thus did the idea of measuring or weighing anything at all become almost incomprehensible to me. It was an idea from Flatland grocers surely, said my mother. Who but Flatlanders would want to weigh and measure things throughout all the dread days of their miserable Flatland lives?

This, as I conceived it, was a profound example of what some call a cultural difference. I mentioned it as a kind of joke to one of the Flatland crones who tried to teach me history at Oxford University. This young androgyne was a typical Rubik's Cube full of railway timetables of the Flatland Mind. She turned her grim face away, saying "such thoughts won't get you objectively politicised." She made off quickly into a chill Oxford mist, the social-scientific section of *The Guardian* tucked firmly under her arm.

It comes as no surprise to most people when I tell them that I am not a reporter proper. Whilst such DSS charity was welcome, the work given to me by *The Brentford Sceptic* was not. As a creature out of time, as it were, I find it quite impossible to undertake the common roles and functions of a typical Mechanical Person. Chains of cause and effect, concepts of input and output are all quite beyond me, hence my present unfortunate state.

In later life I had similar problems with Flatland cultural mores. For instance, I didn't understand cricket, The News at Ten, or Cliff Richard songs. Neither did I understand Flatland Royalty. One day they appeared as Admirals, the next as Generals, the next as Air Marshalls, though most of them are as militarily qualified as are Dhobi Wallahs on the banks of the Ganges.

The Ape and Parcel is my local watering hole. This is a typical planetary clearing house full of fallen heroes and escapees such as I, all either mad, bankrupt or exhausted. I suppose that the profuse and timeless chatter in this cosmic refuge has not changed since the days of Shakespeare's *Boar's Head Tavern* in Eastcheap.

Most in *The Ape* have foregone that harness-tasking of science and blessed reality-gaming beloved of far more sensible folk. Some have escaped connectivity, others have escaped organisation, and a gifted few have escaped meaning, mechanism, and especially profundity, thus avoiding the mass murder implied therein.

It is in *The Ape* that I meet what I term the Viewers. I call them that since almost all talk there is about "what was on the telly last night," as it were. Since I do not have an idiot's lantern, and live in what the nineteenth century would call a "doss house," the quaffing Viewers regard me as a rather odd person. Consequently, I am looked upon as someone who can be fed with any kind of old tall tale, if only to see what I can do with such things. One young leftish social-psychiatrist told me that he privately measured what he called the rate and depth of my absorption and rejection of wild stories as a measure of something he called the *real*, a somewhat modern concept (I told him) of which I was hardly aware. I pointed out the mascara on his fluttering lids, and to some local hilarity, told him to piss off to *The Pink and Percy* across the Talbot

Road, where he would find plenty of like-minded reality-macaroons to lick it all off and made him at least look like a decent citizen, even if he was nothing of the kind.

In an ensuing conversation about Royalty, Joan, a young female Viewer, happened to tell me that Royal uniforms were "symbolic." My reply was that I didn't quite know what she meant by that. If I thought I was an Admiral and dressed like one, I said to her, I could be arrested and put away. She replied that that was because people believed in Royalty, and nobody believed in me. I asked her why was this so, Whereupon Mabel, a pink-tinted Essex *chav* of the first football waters, weighed in.

"Because nobody has any kind of trust in you, Mensche."

"And why not?"

"Because you have absolutely nothing to offer."

"But that's the whole idea."

"Idea of what?"

"Aristocracy. I am an aristocrat, not a tradesman. We don't DO anything. But just you wait, Mabel, you'll be happy soon, I am about to fall from grace once more."

"Can't fall from anywhere, you. You're at the bottom."

"Just you wait. I have a feeling that I am about to reach Prime Time."

"The loo's that way. Give us a ring when you've got there."

Laughter all round, of course.

"Get your knee-pads ready Mabel, because when I *arrive* you'll need to do a lot of worshipping."

"I'd rather suck a dog's dick."

"All expression is desire."

After taking a full five seconds to interpret that, Mabel advanced upon me with her fists clenched. Fortunately the pony-tailed mathematician Albert Jones (the apple of Mabel's eye) saved the situation by taking her attention away from her target. Jones is yet another Viewer typical of the customers of *The Ape*: he once said (with a twinkle in his eye) that my "peculiar condition" (as he and most other Viewers call it) was caused by *lack* of exposure (would you believe), to TV.

Much laughter ensued, and indeed, some congratulations followed, when I revealed that I had only ever seen the *thing* (as some call it) for a few seconds whilst passing shop windows. Jones added a comment I am sure he got from my editor, Price, a frequent visitor to *The Ape*:

"You're like that record-breaking African prostitute, Mensche. A hundred thousand customers but not yet irradiated."

"You are so kind, Jones."

Laughter all round, again. I countered by telling the assembled Viewers that although they were all once Shakespeare, so to speak, now they were as near to Shakespeare as the modern Egyptian *fedayeen* are to the original folk of the Pyramids.

This did not go down well.

Focusing on Mary (a very pretty Viewer) I told her that one of my problems with Flatlanders such as she was that they insisted on producing John Pilger-type social-democratic TV documentaries which claimed to show the "reality" of "social situations," adding that I much preferred Hubble photos of the galaxies. At least they, said I, are suitable for bathroom matting or the wallpaper of your local take-away Tandoori. A Communist documentary, by contrast, can only be printed out and used in the toilet.

When Mary said that was exactly what she used them for herself, I regained momentary hope for all who watched that non-cerebral system call TV.

Last Christmas Eve I caused further trouble in *The Ape and Parcel* by asking why scientists and astronomers talked about distant galaxies using the present tense. According to Einstein, said I, the thing we are looking at disappeared many millions of years ago. We have therefore a whole and entire science based on observation of things, which no longer exist. This earned a mock kick-in-the-balls from "scientist" Viewer Mary, and accusations of being something called a *downer* came from anarchist John.

These are just a few examples of what I have to put up with. And what I call the *realists* are the worst. For example, the aforementioned Viewer Mary had one of those concerned and earnest faces that make all socialist women look like prizes from cut-price Christmas puddings. When she opened her mouth it was as if she were announcing a range of fitted kitchens on early morning TV.

"Do you work for a living? Have you ever done anything you are proud of, Mensche?"

"I seduced my Anglo-Saxon tutor's girlfriend at Oxford."

"Disgusting."

"No. Just revenge."

Then Alfred, Mary's battered husband, sallied forth. Like myself, he is an Etonian. As such, I would not put him in charge of the broom cupboard at Madoff Corporation. For the most part, we public schoolboys are now as capable of winning the battle of Waterloo as we are capable of hanging flock wallpaper in a whore's bathroom.

"So you have not done anything of value for the community in your life?" Quoth Alfred.

"I am an aristocrat. I am absolute value. Neither Jesus nor Comet Warehouse has got anything on me."

The mention of the Saviour caused further uproar.

I had to quickly explain that being born and raised a Highland pagan, I had difficulty with the idea of crucifixion as a suitable principle and basis for a moral philosophy. I asked a scholarly priest Viewer (ten pints per night in *The Ape*) how he could be sure that a man who could walk on water was in fact genuinely suffering on the Cross. Being a smart cookie, he said the only crucifixion I should concern myself about was mine own.

I am still trying to form a proper response to his statement.

2. A Bad Attitude

My hundredth social worker in line (rated fifteen pints a night in *The Ape*) said that such views as I expressed represented a "bad attitude" to properly constituted Authority. I replied that my opinions had at least proved useful in some areas. They had enabled me to avoid several decades of the Flatland Arts, Media and Entertainment, which I commonly referred to as the A&F, meaning Arts and Farts.

This got me into more trouble with the minor-league *glitterati* whose watering hole was the *Michael Jackson Disco Bar* of *The Ape*. With half its garish lights shut down because of something called the Recession, no bar service, and peeling posters of Che Guevara and *The Beatles*, it was full of characters who had once had minor parts in minor things such as *Pussy North*, *Mouse Time UK*, the seasonal *Ralph and the Reindeer*, and a popular series called *You Bastards!* I was surprised that none of the performers in this stagnant pool knew the way their profession worked. At twenty-something, they were already tainted animals, paw-marked dolls, sundered from the image-tribe and ready for memory lane. I did note that there was a goodly number of over-weight hermaphrodites amongst them. They appeared to spend almost their entire lives rehearsing for something or other. Bunty Jones, a down-at-heel computer programmer, said that such folk did not actually *live*, they *auditioned*. This, he added, was a new form of viral life. This view, said he, of the cosmos as limitless *performances* was much better than atoms or molecules.

His opinion impressed me. Perhaps this was the way the world ended, with cartoon gnomes in the foreclosed dark looking for their fix of cartoon roles. Since they were all on many different types of drug, it was difficult to talk to them. I was told by Viewer Vera, a very pretty one-shot veteran of Reality TV, that *You Bastards!* was a black and white grainy-grey "art" work shot by the very last Communist commune in Liverpool. The condescending bitch said it was about the "working class," who were always black and white and grainy-grey in Liverpool. She said (with a twinkle in her low-budget eye), that such films were somewhat difficult to cast in that it was not easy to find lots of "working class" people in Liverpool who were Belsen-thin enough for "reality" (I love that word) and something called "artistic credibility." Much sneering mirth ensued when I admitted to having seen three such club-footed Flatland films (the Viewers all loved the phrase) in my life. These films, said I, all featured an actor by the name of Attenborough-Dimbleby. This produced a response immediately from a clutch of junior thespian wannabes led by the waggish Viewer Peter, who informed me (without blushing) that this same said Attenborough-Dimbleby had been in every British film ever made.

Viewer John weighed in by telling the entire *Ape* assembly that this same said Attenborough-Dimbleby was the man who created the "Zoo and Coronation" programmes for BBC television. He is the person, claimed John, apparently chosen by the Top Flatlanders to announce the death of us all, should the Hun get restless again, or the Iranian premier Aboo-Derby (I can never pronounce or spell his name) goes apeshit, and releases his missiles upon poor Israel. By the way, that is a country for which I have the most profound affection, if only because as distinct from Flatlanders, they have something to live for.

In my frequent nightmares, I imagine the Attenborough-Dimbleby cricket-playing face telling us all to go quietly to the shelters before Armageddon, whilst the National Anthem plays through old Civil Defence loudspeakers.

I told Viewer John of my very first experience of what Viewers in *The Ape* call A&F, meaning Arts and Farts. This was seeing (by pure accident) an old black and white film of Shakespeare's play, *Hamlet*. I chose this particular cinema not because I wanted to see the wretched film, but because the back row of the upper balcony offered a good opportunity to plunge my tongue deep into the mouth of my girlfriend at that time, one Lucy Springett. Before active use of said tongue, I caught a few shots of a man (presumably) on the screen (the *Granada* Tooting, actually) in a powdered wig and tights. This Flatland thespian had a chalk-white face, a camp voice, and minced about something 'orrible, or so said my butler Jamison, seated downstairs in the 50p seats. I should add that I could afford staff at that time, as this was before my fall in life, about which more in due course.

I told Viewer Brian (the Cat's Meat Man from the Talbot Road) about this dreadful A&F experience. He responded by claiming that this periwigged figure was the self-same Attenborough-Dimbleby I had previously mentioned to the assembly. He added with a cat's meat twinkle in his eye that I was lucky to have caught the said bounder in the full flower of his youth. Since Brian told a lot of strange stories, I didn't know whether to believe him or not.

Anyway, I continue my tale of a dread night in Tooting. After three minutes, and just when my tongue was getting ready for action, the wretched projectionist had a heart attack and died there and then, would you believe. The manager at once came to the front of house and asked those who did not want to give their ticket money to the widow to raise their hands. Promptly Lucy and myself raised our mitts, and a scowling clerk put one pound fifty into both our young hands.

With much booing from the rest of the audience, we left *The Granada* never to return and I did not see another British attempt at A&F cinematics for some time.

These thoughts now open memory lane for me. Five years after my Tooting experience, and after many other adventures, I was at *The Shepherd's Bush Empire* with another likely lass, Debra Foxton. I remember her in particular because getting stockings and suspenders on a Catholic girl required the skills of a psychiatrist, a wrestler, and an experienced Newgate Turnkey. The poor girl thus reluctantly attired, I was about to nibble her left earlobe when the same Attenborough-Dimbleby person (in short pants) appeared chasing cloned dinosaurs. I returned to Debra's ear, but after three minutes, following a loud explosion in the balcony above, everyone fled, including Debra. Some Irish person was led out handcuffed, screaming about British exploitation or some such tedious thing. As the place was soon on fire from stem to stern, and the manager was screaming from a pre-war stucco balcony at a reluctant fire extinguisher, I decided this was not the time to try for another refund. I wrote countless letters to Eric Tann at Moss Empires about this, month after month for many years.

I have yet to receive a reply.

Ten years later I was at *The Empire*, Leicester Square. The aging Attenborough-Dimbleby was this time in long trousers, and performing something to do with D-Day, Dunkirk, or perhaps the Battle of Britain or the Arnhem landing. I was later told by Viewers in *The Ape* that, as so often with British films, it is hard to tell the difference.

On this occasion I was with the delectable Maggie Flaunceton, but any chance of enterprise on my part was stifled because of a gun battle which broke out in the front row between armed police and some tur-

banned Turks or other. Watusi, Kikuyu or Taliban — I could not tell
which they were. All I knew was that they were screaming about something or someone called Ella, or some such thing. A woman dressed like
a nun wielded an anti-tank rocket-grenade and screamed that this religious sect of hers wanted their boring freedom from some even more
boring thing or other.

The delectable Flaunceton fled immediately and since she was delectable, I fled after her, Kalishnikov rounds pouring over my head and
the wretched Attenborough-Dimbleby person still fighting the Battle
of Britain or something like it above me on the screen.

Since in the melee I lost my ticket, my chance of a refund on this
occasion was nil. Frankly, after that last episode, I couldn't wait to get
home to the Tabernacle Powis Square and hot cocoa, after putting one
of Mrs Cranston's steak and kidney pies into the Baby Belling. I am
happy to say, however, that some years later, after much correspondence
with the Privy Council no less, I received a postal order for £2.68 (new
money) as a refund.

However this was £1 (new money) short of the sum required, and
it led me into yet another period of protracted correspondence with
both Management and Privy Council concerning exchange rates and
refunds old and new.

This last brush with Flatland cinema reminds me of the day some
young English Communists (remember them?) stormed and took over
the old public lavatories in Paddington Station. After declaring the creation of an urban Soviet, and after three foodless days, an attempt was
made to lure out these young free radicals with an offer of free egg, sausage and chips from a mobile van paid for by the Transport and General
Workers Union and the Police Benevolent Fund Charity. The terrorists
complained that the food was not organic, whereupon they were given
Mr. Christian's GM muesli and the early morning issue of the *Guardian* Gay Arts Supplement. This appeared to calm them all down. After
a few mentions in *Time Out* and *The Brentford Sceptic,* never were they
seen or heard of again.

Now these foreign religious nuts we have here now are much more
boringly serious than what used to be called the radical chic of the

Flatlands. The towel-heads should learn about revolution from the Flatlanders, who (thankfully) are rarely serious about anything at all, witness the bits of the A&F I have just mentioned: their revolutions finish up suspended between a Technicolor spew in a Marks & Spencer doorway and a punch-up in your local Taj Mahal take-away on Saturday night.

3. Adventures in Real Time

Being highborn, I have no concept of the profit or advancement that the middle-class Flatlanders crow about. I have also similar difficulty with those rationalisations that comprise the concept of time passing. Even greater is my difficulty with the rather grubby Flatland idea about organising to a particular end or practical purpose. In addition, ideas which relate to such things as mechanical efficiency and commercial skill, I find either recherché or incomprehensible.

As such, primal communication with tradesmen becomes often difficult, as I do not understand pricing and profits. No more do I understand why Flatlanders watch their unspeakably awful television: surely the reason why young men shoot at screens and images on the campus or in the supermarket, there being not a great deal of difference now between any of these things.

It could be predicted that, possessing what my mother calls the Higher Disturbance, as far as any kind of bourgeois success in life was concerned, I was career-bound for disaster. In the course of many a personal, social, business and financial débâcle, I lost every so-called "concrete" financial asset that I ever had. No use, of course, trying to explain to Bailiffs, credit companies and bankruptcy courts that I was not born to deal with solidity in any form.

As I tried to explain to barristers, social workers and Judges, my problem was that, being born an aristocratic entity, I was a prime fall guy and sucker for every pan-dimensional game in the book. In vain did yours truly plead before the High Court, who wanted the last of my money, property and lands. Telling august Judges that my vision of the cosmos was purely ethereal had little effect: it did not impress the Law, riddled with lower-case meritocrats, and tarred with all kinds of corrupt social-democratic modernism. I told my legal persecutors that I knew not linear perspective, never mind measurement, and still less did I understand the concept of monetary or material gain.

Being practical burghers of the city, they could hardly sympathise with a being from what one condescending left-liberal dog-bollock of a lawyer had the nerve to call a "cultural twilight." The reaction was typical. Each Flatland person was either social-scientific-democratic (as they say), Left-liberal, or (horror of horrors!) all these things combined. As such, they had no concept of the aristocratic condition proper.

All these things meant that I cartwheeled my way to financial disaster in a spectacular fashion. My entire inherited fortune was lost through investing in fuel-less motors, alien communication devices, and expeditions to try and find a lost Lemurian civilisation living in the hollow earth under the polar icecaps. Hundreds of thousands of pounds I lost, supporting a trip to Mars in a reverse-engineered flying saucer, brain replacement surgery, and several Yeti and Bigfoot expeditions. I financed time-travel devices to past and future, rockets to the stars, and reincarnation engineering involving occult resurrections of the famous. I poured further vast amounts of money into instant-invisibility ideas, levitation schemes and "living without food" projects.

Such was my reputation for gullibility that one man even tried to gull me into supporting a scheme to stop young girls masturbating. One Arthur Marlestone, a canny Flatland hero of Notting Hill, reckoned that when young women stimulated themselves, there was a danger to ships and aircraft, and to all such relatively fragile things as satellites, space ships and Web networks. Any fractures, breakdowns, crashes and collapses were all due in the main to the orgasmic peak of pre-pubic women which, according to Arthur Marlestone, caused all round cosmic instability.

Apparently this philosopher managed to get his paper considered by the Amenities Committee of Brentford County Council. His picture appeared also in *Exchange and Mart* (but that was for his "Lentils Beat Lust" campaign). His was practically the only stupid project with which

I refused to become involved — although that was not appreciated by dismal minds when I forwarded it as a job reference.

I still have some regrets. The one thing I missed out on was the Meredith Thong Kettle. This was a small kettle big enough to hold a mug of water. It was designed by Cyril Meredith, a typical waster of my acquaintance, and it was intended for "quick, efficient and private boiling of women's thongs." It used solid fuel, and (as Cyril said in his *Exchange and Mart* advert), "it could also make a quick cup of tea in estranged circumstances if carefully scoured out." For once I thought I had cleverly dumped a time-wasting maniac until the Defence Ministry rang Cyril and ordered 100,000 for the Armed Forces, making Cyril a rich man.

My end came when, after supporting an advertising campaign to show that the Queen of England was an extraterrestrial lizard, several Neighbourhood Watch groups warned me that my abode would be torched and I with it if I did not disappear from the district immediately.

During my fall from such ethereal regions to mundane Earth, I did however acquire a few of what the more vulgar Flatlanders call fighting skills. These were mostly nefarious, such as the Ignoble Art of Blackmail. I used this only rarely in self-defence, or at least that's my excuse. Crime, I suppose, is the last resort of a complete whole-earth inadequate such as I, who cannot knock in a nail or do what the lower classes call "an honest day's work."

But again I failed. Even in the rather elementary craft of forced coercion, I simply was not vicious enough. I was such a ninny the quick, sharp-eyed, double-dealing Flatlanders laughed in my face, knowing that I was not evil enough to hurt a flat hair on their nasty two-dimensional heads.

As time went by, however, I grew a little stronger in this application, if only because it was a leisured occupation suitable to my background. I used my skills not for gain, so much as to provide a little food, accommodation, and the luxury of a small private income quite invisible to the beloved Authorities.

Sympathising with my victim, I offered in exchange my company and conversation as a spiritual solace for their loss, but invariably this was refused.

At first it was easy. I carried out no investigation or research, merely hinted in few words that there might be something in a person's life that they might not want others to know. Since this is true of every life without exception, my hints showered money over my head, but only for a very short time.

Needless to say, even this brief success of mine was doomed to failure. Those I was trying to blackmail grew defences as a rotten apple grows mould. In that short time the last house I owned suffered an arson attack and was burnt down. My last car was petrol-bombed, and I was threatened both publicly and anonymously with polonium-poisoning, strangulation, garrotting and shooting (in that sad order). I was so harrassed and pursued by criminals and hired mobsters that I gave up the blackmailing business after a few months.

After the Tantric Heroes of *The Church of Aphrodite* in the Elmbourne Road took my last penny, so to speak, I fell like Milton's Satan to that lake of burning sulphur in Camden Town which goes by the name of *The Salvation Army Last Chance Depot*.

Eventually I was transferred to *The W11 Margaret Thatcher DSS Bed and Breakfast Module* in the Tabernacle, Powis Square. This is known as the "Final Solution House" by DSS "zecs" such as myself, to use a term of Solzhenitsyn; as an expression of social-scientific affections, perhaps the great novelist might have appreciated the word "module."

4. Hoi Polloi as Landscapes of Time

I now return once more to my recent train journey, which all these thoughts of my life had quite vanished away. Ever since rail travel began, it has aroused thoughts of all kinds of mystical journeys. Novels are full of descriptions in which a journey by rail becomes an adventure in time and culture. Both Proust and Forster wrote about such journeys as if they were magic lantern travels in the style of Alan Fournier in *Le*

Grand Meaulnes.

A perfect still-life setting, thought I. Apart from a clergyman curled up like a Tenniel dormouse a few seats away, and his two young girl charges, sipping *Sprite* and reading a pink journal which can only be described as a breviary of poo, pop and pudding, there was no-one else in the carriage. Upon reaching Watford, however, my enchanted voyage into the past was vanished by an approaching mass chorale of *Torremolinos* and *Viva Espania* and other droll chants of what my mother called the Flatland *dervishes.*

In a heartbeat, my perfect setting for unfettered philosophic contemplation went bang down the river of dreams. A screaming struggling football crowd many hundreds strong swarmed into every inch of space in the carriage; they sneered, spewed, farted, wrestled; made lewd remarks to the two young girls, who fled to the Guard's Van on the arm of the somewhat baffled clergyman.

Of course as part of the supposed joke, *The Sceptic* had given me money for Second Class only. I tried to hide from the Flatland groundhogs in the empty First Class, from which a grim-faced commissar promptly ejected me. Back in the ballast and steerage decks, peasant noise obliterated all thought: film stars, media stars, game shows and things called personalities became green blooming image-algae in the brain. Clowns, acts, performances, shows, entertainment jingles and everlasting chat about last night's prog on the *thing* — they all poured out from a score of different technologies, absorbed by hundreds of kidnapped mentalities. Every second groundling clutched what I believe is termed a *ghetto-blaster*, though according to my two girlfriends (of whom more later), this phrase is terribly out of date.

I fled to a tiny grotto in the rattling corridor by the loo, in order for the noise of the product hatchery be minimised. Pushing me aside as an almost-invisibility, the mob came and went, carrying their chanting diddy-boxes with them for life support. They bought, sold, believed and viewed, all whilst evacuating their fluids and solids in a tiny cubicle at eighty miles per hour. Jingles, nursery rhymes, slogans, the very expression of their seething miasma, their dream-machines split the jocund air asunder fore and aft of the narrow loo door.

I could not understand a word of what they were saying. They spoke pure television-pidgin. All I could make out was a kind of tribal chant, rhyming with the motion of the train; it went something like this:

Didjer see that programme last night?
Didjer see that programme last night?
Didjer see that programme last night?

In a moment of inspiration (which told me I was still alive) I supposed that image withdrawal would see Image Riots replace the traditional mob disturbances over food, clothing, money and accommodation. "The people want their images" would be a new cry of history. These Flatland baubles were as essential to the health of non-cerebrals as medical care. In time, thought I, such warbles and chants would replace old molecular treatment and medication, for here there were hardly molecular beings any longer. They were more programmable software than independently corporeal. A new jig, a fresh warble, a new series, and they all twitched into life like plucked strings.

Pushed up against the loo door, the thought came to me that here I was seeing the health-and-care future, where ailments could be re-imaged as a form of cures rather than being blasted by the almost useless "factual" nets of the scientific mechanists. Soap plots and story-technologies would replace surgery and hospitals. No facts or formulations. Just an image voyage into a story landscape of infinite robotic extent.

I supposed poor Marx would weep if he could see his liberated, vastly overweight proletariat drowning in a sea of toys with only nursery rhymes as a doctrine of nature. I noticed none were loners. This was mass bird-flight. Take away tribal chatter and flutter and I supposed they would scream, go into consumer withdrawal, with wired-in commercial breaks sticking out from their robot heads like springs from broken alarm clocks.

Crushed and breathless, to this crowd I was Bigfoot, or Nessie, a half-seen fragment leaving no consumer trace. I myself might not have been noticed, but as soon as they saw my laptop computer under my arm, they made a beeline for it.

Now here let me explain something. Every person on DSS even if they are insane, blind, deaf, or perhaps even dead, is these days given a hand-cranked "green" computer. This is universally termed *The Bangladeshi*, in honour of the country of that name, They were designed originally for that country, and *The Bangladeshi* is a text-only computer. It is just about capable of recieving and sending emails, and naught else. Since no-one who worked for a living would be seen dead with a hand-cranked *Bangladeshi*, any person seen with such a thing was known immediately to be in receipt of what used to be termed National Assistance. This meant of course that they were treated with less respect than a drunken bozo in your five-and-ten-cent store.

The green *Bangladeshi* was the ultimate social stigma. To be seen carrying such a thing under the arm (worse: winding the battery-charging handle whilst the thing was on one's lap) was to endure being treated as an outcast. Women with children avoided me, patrol cars slowed down every time they saw me at my hand-crank on a street corner or a park bench. I have endured screams of "get back to Africa," and from tower block windows noxious substances and liquids have been poured upon me.

Mugs and towels, cars and briefcases are stolen, but never a *Bangladeshi*. In Europe they're used as bookends and doorstops. In Australia the hurling of the *Bangladeshi* had replaced dwarf-throwing competitions. Left behind everywhere, they were disposed of like polystyrene coffee cups. Left on seats in buses or parks, not even the Bomb Squad bothered with them. Not a single one ever made it to a Lost Property Office.

I did not care much, therefore, when a twenty-five stone proletarian balloon full of poo, pop and pud seized my *Bangladeshi* and threw it across Platform Six of Crewe Station, where a crowd was watching an enormous suspended video screen. The cursed instrument soared over their heads, knocking out the TV eye of something called Gay Cooking for Summer Revels. The effect of the suddenly blank screen was devastating. No less than seven Flatland families of five colours and four social conditions, sprinkled with a veritable cocktail of IQs, were rendered imageless for a short deprived moment, and stood panicking and baffled. God help us, thought I, if we ever have to face the Hun again.

Meantime, still pressed against the seething commode, I tried to remain sane by reading Max Simon Nordau's *Degeneration* behind a local newspaper. However, the mob soon caught sight of my book and, enraged, they chased me into the guard's van, where a nice official locked the door. Their determination to Lynch a Literate (which would have made a great popular headline) was not great. Soon they all lurched back to their mini-screens which quite vanished myself and my books as events in time.

Yet, thought I over a welcome cup of tea with the guard, yet I belonged. I was still a moral creature. I would go to war for these barbarians, dive in the sea to rescue them, wish them well at Christmas; I would defend their Rights, their innocence, as much as I would help to feed, protect and educate them.

But this was moral affection, not emotional. Caste was a much deeper thing than class distinction. It meant obligations existed long before birth and long after death. Class could change in a generation — caste was dinosaur bedrock.

I had a bit of a gulp when, stopping at Rugby, I saw a supporter's mob on the platform, sporting tartans of all kins. They faced a screaming Flatland mob of leather-jacketed skinheads, all baying for blood.

This was a low point for me. I was a tartan leader, yet here I was, cowering in hiding with two young girls and a priest. Somewhere in history I had lost command.

Sounds of battle now came from the train carriages as drunken tribes tried to join the riot on the station platform. The guards checked the door locks and listened to police instructions on their mobiles as I sat with the two very frightened young girls and the equally frightened vicar. Mercifully, the train staff served tea all round yet once more as the train moved off.

I asked the younger girl if she would like to hear me read some poetry. She might have been interested had not her suspicious older friend pulled her away from myself as a lone male almost three times her age. Alas, the world was now replete with hatred and suspicion. It couldn't be talked to any more. If a man could not read poetry to a young girl, then as some believers say, the End was Probably Long Nigh.

For the rest of the journey, the clergyman sat between myself and the girls as if the very mention of poetry to young girls was a mortal sin.

Received at Euston Station by massed ranks of police officers, I arrived back in London just as useless, impractical, and as stupid as I had departed earlier in the day. I was suspended, I felt, between all kinds of social and intellectual jokes in a nutrient of universal waste. I visualised my soul as a hangman's noose in freeze frame.

With this image in mind, I bought an ice cream for personal consolation, and stood for a few minutes watching the many fights and arrests as the mob poured off the train. My *Bangladeshi* thrower, I was pleased to see, received special treatment from the Plod, with blood pouring from his head.

Perhaps even he had learned something.

As if Nature were enjoying this scene, over the melee hung an illuminated strip referring to a Chinese earthquake. It read A MILLION DEATHS.

Below surged many more dead than that. These dead would burn libraries, museums, watch aristocrats' heads flop into baskets, and the final obscenity was that I cared, which was the ultimate absurdity. Like mouth-less insects, the mob were born without the brains to last for even a summer's day, and yet I cared for them. They had the same flaps of skin and bone I had, the same poverty, the same madness. Understanding this took away my ability to hate. It was one of the few things I was proud of: it meant that I was still fully alive. If a man hated, he was more dead than he could ever believe.

With such mad thoughts in mind, I headed for my equally absurd home.

two

The Margaret Thatcher DSS Bed & Breakfast Module

1. Subsistence as Art Form

THE TABERNACLE facing Powis Square was once an ancient Wesleyan church, and uniquely circular in construction. Long abandoned by its original owners, it was taken over by the local Kensington and Chelsea Council some twenty years ago. It contains now a "temporary" nest of hardboard divisions occupied by what I once heard one of my beloved social workers describe as "the lowest level of incurable malingerers" such as myself. As that is a somewhat curious description of a certain section of Mankind, I feel obliged to tell you something here and now. Whenever I move into a new DSS doss-house (this ancient Poor Law term being still current amongst the *zecs,* escapees, and welfare *cognoscenti*), I obey my perfect pedigree of instinct. I do what all top *zecs* do. First I get the lights fixed, hire staff, and I then find myself some really nice pieces of what some wasters call "best hot pussy."

Let me tell you now that following such chieftain instincts, I have formed a moderately representative family for the *Margaret Thatcher DSS Bed and Breakfast Module.* The two still-dreaming nubiles by my side are my bosom-friends: Betty "Shackster" Baxter, from darkest Africa, and Countess Svetlana Romanov, from darkest Europe.

Forty-five-year old Countess Svetlana (now pulling on her purloined *Agent Provocateur* pants), masquerades as my elder sister for the
purposes of DSS certification. She is something like twentieth contest-
ant in line for the soon to be (thank the gods) restored Romanov dynasty. Eighteen year old Betty "Shackster" Baxter (now tucking into an
equally purloined breakfast), masquerades as an adopted daughter of
the Countess.

We are watched over by the ever-curious ex-corporal "Fishpot" Cart-
er (MC and Bar), Assistant Module Team Manager. He often snarls
vile Parachute Regiment curses at the respective members of my extended family, mostly whilst on the rounds of his early morning pussy-
glancing and corpse-checking duties. He once said to me that going to
bed with both an elder sister and that elder sister's adopted daughter
simultaneously and getting the DSS to pay for the revels must entail
getting the paperwork exactly right.

Whereupon the Countess stressed to the good corporal that we always take care to feed the rule-drones well. Keep the prole-clerk's coats
sleek with salacious curiosity, she said in her natural Marlene Dietrich
tones, and you don't hear much from the wondrous things. Young Betty
weighed in, in her Willesden tones, saying that all the old lefties were
wrong about Authority. If you feed it like a horse, said she, you can put
it out to grass happy as a house brick, and occasionally use it to pull and
heave the heavy pack loads when you take your intimate *caravanserai* to
its next appointment with Welfare State destiny.

For myself, I pointed out to Fishpot (then ruefully retreating with
his mop, his bucket, and his Regiment oaths), that we were all pieces of
authentic twenty-first-century *Meccano*. I added that as such, only *The
Margaret Thatcher DSS Module*, Svetlana's title, Betty's blackness, the
twenty-four hour combined screwing, the fortnightly benefit, and his
experience of knocking out three T-55 tanks in Gulf War 1 were what
any organ grinder's monkey would call *real*.

This ancient piece of Terry Wogan Britain (I always judge people by
what TV era they were spawned in) sang eighties commercial jingles,
and was a prime informer to the Police and DSS. Regarding my nubiles,

he always gave me an old soldier's look, and said that if I needed any help at any time, I had his mobile number.

My only indulgence other than limitless naked female flesh is a domestic servant. That absolutely essential sign of good breeding and address comes in the form of *Manang* Ratcher, our maid and cook. Times may be hard, but lower than a single servant I refuse to sink.

Some might say that *Manang* Ratcher's arrival in this sceptred isle, lashed to the back-axle of a Leyland twenty-five-tonner full of frozen coolie-bread bound for Bradford, was not the most auspicious qualification for domestic service. Nevertheless, she has now secured a respectable position, though she has to do our shopping in full Muslim drag in order to avoid surveillance by those of yeomen sentiment who would force her back beside the old Moulmein Pagoda faster than you can say multicultural. Though her "quarters" be only a blow-up mattress twixt clothes-horse and sink, still her presence suffices to make my household stand out socially from the snoring, cursing lower orders in the surrounding hardboard divisions.

The only other thing I live with is a permanent note in my head of the exact location of the nearest tall building, should I, in the midst of all this splendour, finally decide to go ask God why I carry around the bonus prize of pictures of soap stars in my head, which is my only point in common with the peasantry.

I think I should be told.

Connoisseurs of the forces of destiny will by now have concluded I am as well equipped for battle or adventure as any cosmic voyager of past, present and future. In true anti-heroic mould, I have no food, no money, no belongings, and most deliciously important of all, absolutely no hope. Not that I would ever be so silly as to allow any helpful constructive social-democratic Viewer to give me friendly suggestions as to how to improve my lot. Neither would I want anyone to think even for a minute that I am ever going to search for anything that will in any way create any kind of moral or social rehabilitation within me. Should I ever have the misfortune to attain grace, honour, or even dignity, I will immediately take it to the nearest Sony showroom and leave the malformed manikin to applaud itself to death before fifty simultaneous channels.

That is because I am not silly.

Such a discovery would presuppose Meaning, and you don't need to be on this planet very long to know that Meaning means Labour. And you don't have to have known me, George Mensche, for very long to work out that I do not intend to do or carry out so much as a cat's cradle of any job, deed, task, mission, or role. Neither do I intend to contribute in the slightest to whatever is the current pose and mask of the directed motivations of humanitarian causes, positive directions, healthy attitudes or creative responses. Further, I do not seek any purpose, advancement or praise. Still less do I desire any fruition, transcendence, victory, or triumph. But above all (and I speak also for my two lovely partners), I do not want any solutions — intermediate, plausible or final.

All I want this morning is what is properly termed a "Controversial Family Reassessment Form," and a nice pen to sign it with. After pressing that particular Button B of the Social Services panel, and having downed a good stiffener of *Tree-Frog* in *The Ape and Parcel*, I shall be ready to resume that great monkey-in-the-spaceship game called life.

We are now being swilled down in our unique three-person zinc-tank by the *Manang*. Out we step, the *Manang* hands us sackcloth, and brings tea. I open Huysman's *Against Nature*, and prop it against a shadowy loop of my pseudo-sister's nakedness entwined with that of her pseudo-daughter. This morning, after a night like last night, I need a kick-start towards the path of true philosophy like the lower orders need *Big Breakfast Soap Hour*.

The Countess Svetlana is a great beauty. She looks like the young Veronica Lake of the old films. I am ashamed to say that I am utterly unable physically to protect her from endless suitors, but the few brave enough to cross the water-barrier of the Grand Union Canal and penetrate our native quarter are usually seen off by the faithful *Manang* Ratcher, a dab-hand with the thrown half brick and the short Saipan fish-harpoon.

Sometimes when I see Svetlana in a column of light from the open door, taking out liberated vegetables from the lining of her long Gannex, I am consumed by bourgeois lusts, and would like to buy her a white fur coat and photograph her coming out of some world-famous French hotel. Though I cure myself of these occasional lapses into vulgar sensibility, I do wish I could return the affection that I receive. These two beauties mend a button on my shirt, they smile at me, touch me, and make tea and toast for me, but all I ever see within individuals is the flow of history and conflict, the clash of epoch and idea, the structure of symbols and the self-generating flux of ever-evolving structures of natural advertising. Most of the time I hate this ability. I would like to be able to see unique individuality. In this respect I would like to return (in the proper consumer-religious sense), the love of these two unique women who do a combined sucking of my cock and balls such as would bring down the walls of old Jericho.

Therefore what I love about Svetlana is some great historical identity, rather than a person. I sense many of those huge icebergs of dream just below the surface-sense of her ticking brain. Whenever Svetlana hears Lehar or Strauss, she so quivers with near-teleportation that she looks about to vanish there and then. She freezes — stands quizzical, as if the horns of elfland sound to her, and as if she vaguely knows that somehow she has wandered too far away from the forest, and doesn't quite know how she will ever get back. Betty says she wouldn't be surprised if Svetlana disappeared one night forever from us, just as something like a crumpled blonde swan in a beautiful gown falls into the middle of some great swirling masked ball of old Moscow or Vienna, to the astonishment of befrogged dynasties.

I reckon that only the thinnest of perceptions separates her from the networks of jostling ancestors within. Sometimes she seems even afraid herself that a mere sudden change of mood would catapult her to the wooden deck of a heaving sailing vessel where she would lie, terrified, looking up at some equally baffled crew, their backs to an ancient sea.

Betty is also a great beauty; she is a dead ringer for a globally famous black model but, as distinct from Svetlana, she lives almost completely in the future. Betty's images are new, Svetlana's images are old. Betty, unlike Svetlana, doesn't have to cope with the Somme, or Dunkirk, or even Auschwitz or Hiroshima in her DNA. Practically nothing of her has had anything to do with any of these things. Psychically, she can't be much older than Duke Ellington. Like a modern Topsy, she just crystallised with Little Richard and Tina Turner. Infinite European grief is not hers; she can start afresh, create a possible new Eden with Martin Luther King, Marcus Garvey and Franz Fanon. Betty is a cosmic liferaft. Her race gave the twentieth-century its music, which is a fuck sight more than the white man ever gave it. Betty has a Darwinian chance over Svetlana who is, like Europe, almost dead of the Past. She has centuries of death still inside her, a great procession of mourning families, always close to her, a murmuring host to disturb her nights and days.

Nightly, sandwiched between these two women, supporting many highly-wrought fairy stories by the thinnest of State sanctions and the most transparent of deceptions, I witness the spore-exchange of the myth of Blood with the myth of Entertainment. But I remain only a mere counter of the strands of the helix of the exchange, a stock-taking storeman of impressions and energies. I suspect sometimes I am a robot. I suspect sometimes I am a winding-down reject of some experiment in machine-intelligence long since forgotten by a something which is now beyond the Milky Way. Within my increasingly obsolete circuitry, I am able only to see human beings as systems. When I screw my two wives, I screw the seam between many disintegrating belief-structures all trying to out-masquerade each other.

This I call history.

Svetlana is very conscious of history. Precisely upon the death of each season (such as winter's end, signalled by the E-tab trading on our doorstep acquiring a militant tendency), Svetlana stares into space as if she sees faces. Faces not around anymore, as if she had lost them just after she was born. Not the pampered and preening faces of Betty's new and vibrant Media Trash Culture, but faces cut and faceted like diamonds, old faces of empire and ocean, faces of savannah and plain and forest and mountain, forever calling to her from endeavours somehow incredibly still in continuation. She can recall journeys she has never made, knows people she has never met, can see a half-face in a crowd, rush over, with all those rows of crosses inside her like a great procession, as if to meet a face she knows from some magnificent ball whole generations ago. Sometimes whilst she sleeps, I hear her roaming through those great mandala-houses of the eighteenth century transplanted from the heart of the Rome of Caesar Augustus, just as if they were talismans that held the secrets of her many deaths and transformations.

2. The Narrow Palliasse

These are the details of my troubled life up to the present, or as much as I care to remember. But what now, say you? Well, here I am still paddling up the twenty-first century river in what Flatland Media calls *real time*.

Thus do I view the wide Empyrean in a building which remembers the flogging of matelots, the hanging of unruly maidens, one cold water tap as a Christian gesture and fish-skin condoms thick as shoe leather. At this stage in my twenty-first century journey up-river, my only possessions are an Income Support Voucher mattress, a set of out-of-date Community Fund Milk Tokens, a Euro-Commode full of forged Salvation Army Free Sandwich Tickets, a totally inadequate DSS Trouser Allowance, and two naked nubiles now at their *toilette* whilst squatting on my narrow palliasse.

And they tell me I am one of the lucky ones.

In this illustrious setting did I conclude that a refusal to work is one of the great crimes of history. It is far worse than a refusal to fight, love or mourn. In our own time, a rejection of all labour is worse than a refusal to buy — or a refusal even to view. Long since did I come to conclude that the finding of myriad laborious tasks for such philosophers as myself has always been one of the main objectives of principalities and powers. Many of the great minds of history have spent their entire lives forming impressive theories of just how to create multiple activities for the great partly washed, such as myself.

The phrase *Arbeit Macht Frei* may have been forged on the gates of Auschwitz, but work certainly did not do anything for me. In few places is it recorded that we eternally unclean are forever ungrateful for the fruits of such often brilliant social-democratic theories which are always showered upon us instead of a good and regular supply of food, clothing, money and accommodation, as is due to the high-born by right.

In this place, on my fortieth year to heaven, I await the next due instalments of Nature's Meaningful Grand Design. Yet more cosmic purpose and harmony will no doubt be revealed upon the hour by the forces of Science and Democracy, Enlightenment and Reason. I tremble expectantly before the next Great Leap Forward, the next "scientific breakthrough," or revelations brought about by the New Cosmology.

Those who represent such forces of social and political enlightenment would be pleased to know that my unique family unit is probably the most highly qualified in the Social Security Firmament. Between us there's an MA, a D. Phil, and yours truly with a bad Third in English Literature and Language. Even *Manang* Ratcher claims she is an ex-Luzon University Professor of Physics, here to do her GCSE in Mathematics. We are ever-ready to spread our knowledge. When the *Manang's* finished doing the bed, serving dinner, and polishing what little silver we still possess, the *Manang* gets a free tuition bonus from young Betty.

Come night, Svetlana tries to write a book, Betty squints at American film and music magazines, or transforms a piece of old sacking into something slitted and sequined. Then does the *Manang* kneel by the twin primus, warming whatever animal gels, pastes and crushed powders from forest, field and test tube we must process through our pipes in order miraculously to preserve ourselves in this bubble. We eat under the single provided bulb, some of us with only part of our being in this time and space: snared by a cobweb strung by the machinations of a history not quite dead and not quite born.

Viewers in *The Ape* ask me how I can love two women simultanaeously. I answer by saying that I am as terrified of love as I am of order. Every time I have loved I have been as near death as ever I want to be. The few rare moments of blessed hatred in my life were much less destructive to my being than love. I only rediscover love when I am near chaos, because, like most human beings, I am at my very best when I am utterly terrified. I am only myself when I am in the middle of a disturbance. Only do I know love once more when the dead plaster face of received experience fractures into those disasters which show the essential truth of things.

We now have a VHF scanner. I had a great deal of trouble in getting the DSS to install the aerial on the roof of our module, and often of a night we rush over to the crying wounds of the bleeding city. We speed to the disruption on our liberated *Muddy Foxes*, avoiding all traffic lights to try and arrive before the sirens in order to satisfy ourselves that all is well and instability is thriving. Unlike most, we can only sleep to sounds of battle. Fires, bombs, accidents, anything will do just to disrupt the strutting stage of the mechanised affections. Such true love is brief. It has a short life before the earnest, twitching faces of professionals arrive to take the experience away and claim it as their own. We depart sadly as they rush in with their devices, and their finite causes and effects. Stout, practical, simple-minded lads and lasses, their clear eyes and hefty arms and glistening equipment vanish quickly all the private rites of grief, love and witness.

My relationship with both the Countess Svetlana and Betty is that we three recognise that we all have junk DNA in our make up. We are all functions of waste, absurdity and nonsense. All of us are perfectly happy with this, if no one else is. As an example of a strand of meaningless mind-stuff, the Countess asked me, naturally enough, if I could keep her in the manner to which she was accustomed.

I replied that the only thing I could offer her was my searing ambition to create one of the great Social Security records of this century. Svetlana countered by saying that at least I could say to people that I had not bought my own furniture. To which I teased her about her snobbishness. I won't say she is toffee-nosed exactly, but when she got up the other morning there was a letter for her, and on the envelope in fancy letters were the words: YOU'VE WON! Open it quickly I said, you never know, with a message like that we could all be breaking wind through watered silk come Yuletide. "Would *you* open something which said you've *won?*" she replied. To which I teased her about her meanness. I addded that she would not spend 20p on a coin telescope to see the Second Coming. I told her, she was tight as a kettledrum at an oratorio. And here — as yet another example of what I have to put up with each and every night — here is page forty three from the Countess Romanov's *Dictionary of Junk Truth:*

Evil: Any phrase or sentence with the word "social".

Writer's café: middle-class fantasy.

Ordinary people: The essence of boredom.

Science: Sixth-form lies.

Facts: The ultimate conspiracy.

Contradictions in terms: English Intellectual, Irish porn star, literary writer who has worked in science, industry and technology.

The Ancient World: Time Out magazine, the NASA complex at Houston, Texas.

Commerce & Industry: Auschwitz, Belsen, Dachau, Treblinka, Ravensbruck, I.G.Farben, Seimens, Krupp, and all points East.

German: Psychopathic mass-murderer, torturer, and organiser of cruel medical experiments in extermination camps. Direct cause of over sixty million deaths in the Twentieth Century.

Hell: Democracy, Rationalism and the Left.

Romantic: That immediate post-Giro feel.

God: Somebody who cannot make teeth as good as humans can.

How times change. She left out the Pope, the Environment, and Men in Knickers on Channel Four. And I say to her, will it sell? Betty is equally as creative. Three nights a week she goes out and does her one-woman show, *Nature as Fraud*. Done with fireworks, naked pole-dancers and lots of exotic animals, Betty's show is quite a bash, I can tell you. It's a kind of dance-rap-rant based on invented quotations. Here is some of it:

Objectivity means that you have not done what you have just done.

Rather trust a scream from Britney Spears than a database from the trading class.

I always prefer the fictions to the facts. They tell me a hell of a lot more.

Don't kill Muslims — turn them into customers.

America invented Pleasure, and has never been forgiven for it.

When we imagine we create a form of life.

Like a Masturbating Nun, the Sceptic lives in Denial.

Don't follow the money — follow the stage-fronts.

As ritual murder, the scientific commercial break is the most spectacular weapon we will ever see.

Like Hamlet, as soon as the advertisements around you start talking about reality, reach for your sword.

Mundane Claims need Mundane Explanations.

Of course any tyro hearing this stuff will have no problem in guessing correctly that my two wives are first-class media-rejects. Both had their own TV programmes before being doused like bad smells. The Live sex, eating bowls of maggots and pissing on her audience got Svetlana ejected very quickly from Channel Four. In Betty's case she tried to strangle a top BBC executive on stage. He came within seconds of his miserable life before being pulled off by minders, much to the nation's regret.

This admixture of fame and infamy makes for a great sex life. Right in the middle of triangular *coitus*, my pseudo-sister remembers something about truth, my pseudo-daughter remembers something about fraud, and I remember which day I withdraw the DSS Benefit cash for all three of us.

In the words of Warden Sproat (he got the phrase from a French prostitute who leaguers downstairs) it all works magnificently as a junk *ménage*.

three

A Junk Cosmology

1. The Brentford Sceptic

AS I SAID, a few weeks back, under pressure from the beloved Authorities, in order to continue my extended family's Parish Relief, I was forced to take a temporary part-time unpaid job as a journalist on *The Brentford Sceptic*. This publication thrives still, even though I continue to write for it, which is a wonder in its very self.

The Brentford Sceptic is what is known as a give-away publication. The folded crown-sized yellow sheets are mostly full of advertisements, with a sprinkling of local Brentford news, including Sports and Entertainment sections. Occasionally it features a few original topical articles by galley slaves and powder-monkeys such as yours truly.

As such, when looked at not too closely, the paper appears to be a local success story. Advertisers, impressed by the claimed weekly print run of 50,000 copies, pay through their noses for insertions in the hope that the paper will be "distributed" far and wide. But the sub-text, or the "social-scientific reality" as the old Marxist-Leninists used to say, is that the print run is "actually" ten per cent of the claimed run, and only ten percent of that is actually distributed. The remainder is quietly shipped to one Savage Ron, a little man in Bow who does anything and everything equally quietly. As part of a cycle of almost religious intensity and significance, Savage Ron duly pulps the lot behind locked doors. He then sells the pulp to the paper manufacturers who then re-supply the printers of *The Brentford Sceptic*.

As a system of convenience-ecologies I find this process both interesting and admirable.

Sometimes, like most tragic animals, I develop of Theory of Nature. My own Cosmology is based on what I call a Brentford Junk System. Such a System is completely reliant on fantasy-management, as is much else in this world of ours.

The distribution of the paper is a nightly operation that would do credit to the SAS. A score of scallywags fresh from the DSS queues, and grateful for a free late-date tuna sandwich, throw a few hundred copies into late-night superstores. A similar number of copies are hurled into the doorways of closed shops, and the remainder is dumped in parks, canals, hedgerows, and the unswept corners of Cineplex lots and branch railway stations. If there is a girl wearing a thong on the front page (and we make sure there is), by dawn there is not a sign of a single copy, and everybody is happy.

As a holographic virtual structure, such a junk system is capable of rousing a kind of surrogate affection, just as a baby monkey regards a hot water bottle as a nourishing mother. Thus is the impression given that all's well at *The Brentford Sceptic*.

All this I go along with, not just because I need to stop my ribs meeting one another, but because I am a philosopher who fully believes in what I call Unintelligent Design as a Universal Principle. Clever-dicks are always talking about "intelligent" design. But to straighten out our newspaper and make it into an "intelligent" system would lead to ruin. Those slippery elementals called the deities are, like everything else, both cranky and disreputable. At the first hint of rules and regulations the gods smell dinner, and begin to prepare those of good clean intentions for prison, the asylum, or the river with a proverbial small millstone around the neck.

Success or failure is a matter of adjusting perspectives. If a "clean kitchen" came in (such is the phrase), he or she would smash this working structure of corruption and lies to pieces. Some might say that would be a very moral thing to do, but the trouble is that if that happened, as it did with the Communists, then nothing would work any more.

When my Junk Cosmology is discussed in *The Ape*, some of the more perceptive Viewers there call me the New Copernicus. The sublime harmonies that the Arts Supplements play their violins to always annoy me, if only because Adolf Hitler was a far better watercolour artist than anyone will ever allow him to be. This gives moralists a problem in the same way that a right-angled turn at 5,000 mph by an object in the sky gives scientific rationalists a problem.

As I tell them in *The Ape,* my Brentford Junk Cosmos has great beauty. There are no agenda-needles going in. It works this way. Those who are advertising in *The Sceptic* think that their products are reaching wide audiences. Of course it often happens that an advertiser's sales are increased by some means quite independent of *The Sceptic*. Nevertheless, these sales are attributed to the "success" of the paper.

Since the largely trash items as advertised, from bed linen to cars, are equally fantasy-based, my Brentford Cosmology again represents a fantasy-ecology as a management of perspectives, to the benefit of all parties concerned.

This is what I call a Junk System. Far better than the harmony, meaning and purpose that the "scientific" wired-jawed ballet dancers from *The Guardian* talk about. Sensible, well-informed folk are a junk disaster. I don't listen any more to Flatland reason: what I want to know is who, or what, is *running* the inevitable junk-catastrophes of Mind and Spirit both. I want to know: who or what is producing and selling and directing the B-feature flicker-sequence that some call profound knowledge and yet others call *reality*?

Therefore I go for junk. It speaks to me. A particular Flatlander might be talking about mathematical physics or theology but I am interested in who or what is running the rubbish-system that hath him or her in thrall.

I try to get behind the screens of intelligence or protestations of profundity. I go for haircuts and smells, sounds, lights and the atmosphere of the programmed scripts which make up every person. Crap talks to me. It gives me clues to the advertisements and the management suites that constitute a person. I go for acts and productions, for the images that flow from the cartoons.

Of course with such thoughts in mind, it goes without saying that I consider aristocracy to be the most perfect form of universal junk.

2. The Flatland Firmament

On my way to the office of *The Sceptic* this morning, the popular press announced a typical Flatlands start-of-the day programme of the first decade of the twenty-first century. What was called a "large multiplex dysfunctional family" living on some woebegone housing estate in the North of England had come apart at the seams. The popular press carried photos of overweight masses of TV-settee blubber, with Neanderthal faces, piling into police vans, all carrying their bits and pieces in old *Colonel Saunders* doggie-bags. The charges involved rape, murder, incest, drugs, and also criminal deception regarding in the main Social Security Benefits. As a kind of Flatlands media *aperitif*, they were charged also with the selling of child pornography downloaded from the Web.

But the wondrous thing was that in this family net (one typical branch of which included a woman with seven children by five men), there were many famous Flatland yeomen names, including Asquith, Lamb and Drake. These were names that had been embedded in their district for hundreds of years.

This led me to conclude that the very Flatland Firmament was in twain.

I read of this wondrous peasant junket whilst enjoying planetary warming and a cup of coffee outside the Leisure Centre, Brentford, and waiting for the office of *The Sceptic* to open. The start and finish of this one cup of coffee saw a snowstorm, a hail storm, all interrupted by photo-glare flashes of blinding sunlight. This nuclear-blast light (as almost everybody called it), revealed a sky scored with what were called Chemtrails. These were spread at great height by many high-performance aircraft of which the RAF, the government and the airports had no knowledge at all.

I was about ask God if he did all this for a living when I had the dread thought that Bill Price, the long-suffering Editor of *The Brentford Sceptic*, was surely going to send me up to Flatlands North to report on this aforesaid dysfunctioning family morass.

My Editor is a prime *blunt* (as distinct from a bloke) from Wigan North. An ex-bricklayer and veteran Marxist from an era as long gone as Harold Wilson and the Pound in your Pocket, he still talks about something called "social-scientific reality." This weird and wonderful idea, now gone with the check-pattern trousers of Rupert the Bear, masquerades still as a solid consumer-convenience of the Looney Left and socialist *intelligentsia*. To a generation that knew black-and-white TV, Price, as a last piece of extended nineteenth century brickwork, could be put in the window of a grocer's shop where once cheese was cut with a wire and prices marked up with a pencil on torn brown paper bags.

This definitive Flatlander quotes and mimics soap characters in conversation, talks about car insurance, and the price of things called Package Holidays. He was nicknamed "Jordan" because of his puffed-out drink-sodden eyes, for all the world like the breasts of the famous model. After a liquid lunch, these eyes move up and down, and he becomes positively pornographic.

Discussing what he calls pompously "briefings and commissions," he calmly skewers open 600g tins of *Celebrity Pork Roll*, his favourite food, known locally as *hippo-meat*. To the consternation of visitors, he scoops out the disgusting contents with his fingers and throws the pink gunge into his cavernous mouth.

Price rejects almost all my work, saying that it is "highly subjective." When that particular *bon mot* bounces about like a counterfeit cheque, you know you've got a Commie on your hands. On occasion Price makes the observation that it appears that I am not "a man of the people." When I said that I was glad about that, he went into a kind of Marxist *petit mal*, his tit-eyes glowing like vampire orbs.

Like myself, and indeed like most thinking human beings, Price was hung suspended between cartoon and junk cliché. His mind moved between themes and subjects like a carrion crow picking at heads stuck on poles. I see him always covered with old East German engine rust, mixed with the gunpowder of 1870. Given a chance, he still launches into a pre-set speech about Industrialisation and something long gone called the "working class." A recent exchange went like this:

"Now Mensche, what I want to see from you is a piece that is clear, precise and — er — sociological." He swelled with pride at his successful pronunciation. "How about that?"

"You're doing well."

"I want the truth. I want reality!"

"The Communists always said that before they shot you."

"Might have been the best solution in your case."

I quoted Betty back at him.

"Truth and reality do not concern me. I prefer fantasies. They give me a lot more information."

That always caused trouble, thought I. You had to be Real. All over the world they beat you to a pulp until you were converted to Reality. Reality was the most vicious Religion of all. You were made to suck on it as good nymphettes suck on dicks. As for the truth — well, True Believers did even worse things to you until you were converted to Truth. Denial of both at the same time was quicker, more merciful, leading as it did to instant whispering Death. I always thought that Truth and Reality were approximations, myself … however, torturers are not interested in partial confessions. Being the elite of the Flatlanders, they want accuracy; accounts of phenomena must go down to molecular level before they finish the story episodes right there with knife, rope, bullet, or (worse) an *explanation*.

The only thing I knew about explanations was, they made you go away from your target. Explanations were skunk-smoke. I look at all such received concepts of "reality" as would-be worshippers of Keat's "stout Cortez" looked down at their chopped-off wrists.

"Well in that case I don't think we can do business, Mensche."

"Have mercy. I was born before facts were invented. I am still a cave painter. In my animal skin, I am still at the point where it all began to go wrong —"

"Mensche, none of this helps me with all the problems I have with you."

Price dug out a thick slab of pink *hippo* and threw it into his mouth as if throwing a herring to a seal. With his cheeks full, he raised his eyebrows to the ceiling, bit a fingernail, and swallowed a tablet, flushing it down with a gulp. Sighing, he brought the famous tit-eyes down upon me, and banged his fist on his desk. "Mensche, you're sacked."

There and then I decided to offer Price a morsel slipped to me on a wild night in *The Ape*. In such cases of dangerous confrontation, I always bore in mind that even a little bit of illicit knowledge can often be used to bring down dynasties, empires, individuals — and especially, those structures of truth and reality which were after your arse. This commendable result was in large part due to the irresistible antics of those flaps of skin between the legs, tentacles, slime-pods and antenna of every living creature. My personal investigative rule was not "follow the money," but follow the clits and dicks. Follow the fantasies, not the facts. Shakespeare would have understood.

"I didn't know your wife has a third bank account. And neither does the Tax man."

I didn't add, "Or the Serious Fraud Office." That was only if things went really pear-shaped. Price didn't know that I knew that his young wife Bev ran one of the biggest call-girl rackets in Merrie England. Of course I didn't want to go that far. After all, I could be very dead if I did not manage my job security in layers of colour coded threats. It was common knowledge also that *The Brentford Sceptic* was being run as what Jones of *The Ape* called a "dead-bollock" tax loss for Bev's lucrative prostitution business.

In addition, I was withholding from Price my knowledge of his very young boyfriends, too young indeed in many cases. They were supplied by his wife for the mutual amusement of the couple.

"I won't say anything about your younger appetites."

A relieved glance from Price. Sometimes you just had to let people off the hook. I now judged my security state to be YELLOW, which was three down from RED, which meant Murder Imminent. I relaxed. Tonight I'd once again be safe on my palliasse in the Tabernacle, reading passages to my nubiles from Rabelais and De Quincey, safe in the knowledge that I had purchased another day from the gods by means both foul and fair.

Price now disappeared into an interior as deep and inscrutable as any in the most down-at-heel Flatland housing estate. I guessed that he was quietly fuming in some deserted niche, his lips tight and his ex-bricklayer's fists clenched.

This was how things worked at the bottom end of the world. A thinking man had to cut corners on Nature, or She sure cut corners on the thinking man. Everybody covered themselves. Would-be escapees such as myself, who had largely managed to avoid the latter half of the twentieth century let alone the first decade of the twenty first, admired the way in which Nature produced fresh scripts to order faster than skunk-smoke from a bramble-hide. Sometimes the script burst, just like winter ice shattered unlagged pipes, and the world stage became strewn with the corpses of both the living and the dead. What Price called "social-scientific reality" was yet another junk-heap consisting of abandoned scripts, of which Price and myself were just two examples. A particular script worked for a while, just as a car might work for a short time after a bad smash — but you could never be sure what had been damaged under the bonnet.

Of a sudden Price was back. Thirty years of suppressed violence looked me in the eye, With a *Quorn Pseudo Veggie-Pasty* in one hand (the Leisure Centre cafetaria specialised in such), and a red and pink slab of *hippo* in the other, his hod-worn fingers were ready to tear me apart. I shot the threat level back to RED.

Now knuckles white. Clenched fists. Soon, if I did not think quickly, both the *hippo* and the *Pasty* (woven from genetically modified sea-weed), might well be down my throat, and any future ancestors born with three heads and hermaphroditic tail.

"Supposing I smashed you to a pulp here and now, Mensche?"

"Don't worry Price, I won't knock down your family stage-set, and I don't want to die in the name of moral revolution. I prefer a plain honest heart attack in *Tesco's* doorway, if you don't mind. I'll leave you the coupons, so don't worry."

Price looked relieved and his threat level changed to BLUE. Mind you, BLUE still meant serious business.

If the bosses really wanted to play rough, the planet-sized porno-circuits and child sexploitation networks were other B-feature options I could bring into play when a Flatlander like Price was hard to crack. The very thinnest of slices cut from their porno tentacles would do. Hacked from computers and sent first-class registered post in a well ventilated box, as it were, such icons of the discovery of illicit viewing worked wonders. Save of course those who could not give a five-barred fuck in any case, and there were very few of them around. The great Forbidden Fantasy was as deep a magical rite as ever it was. It defied both science and sense, all social-democratic rationalisations, and thus of course agreed with my doctrine of Junk Nature.

People were fundamentally subversive, anarchic. They liked seeing things they were not supposed to see, and thinking thoughts they were not supposed to think. This raising of images ruled the world; it controlled those historically *arriviste* ideas of fact and common sense. Objectivity and Calculation, the two most entertaining sports in the junk ecology. Concrete reason stood no chance against the airless forms of dangerous eroticism, both intellectual and sexual, the most vulnerable spots in the common rationale.

Viewers in *The Ape* had whole directories of addresses of such sensitive spots within the human needs spectrum. Knowledge of these things were used as weapons whenever the beloved Top Hats got out of line. Castles and empires were brought down by the covert discovery that banned images were being secretly gazed upon. That had hardly anything to do with criminality in the conventional sense — it was about magic, sorcery; the image gave a secret power to the human imagination, and oh, that would never do.

3. The Tic Bird and Mr. Blinge

The voice of Price broke my meditation as if my thoughts were registered by some watchful principle, which tried to destroy them immediately.

"Now here's an easy job for a beginner. You go along and interview the Tic Bird. He's that young bloke has sat five years outside the Portobello *Tesco's* with his begging bowl, come rain come shine. Not even you could cock this one up, Mensche."

I could not possibly do the job, of course, but back at the Tabernacle the Countess, who fortunately knew Charlie the Tic Bird well, obligingly wrote a suitable piece for me in ten minutes. As I said, the Countess had presented her own commercial television programme a number of years back, and she had interviewed the Tic Bird when he fronted his own band, *The Toxic Morons*.

After we had transmitted this account by e-mail to *The Sceptic*, we three were soon snoring sound as Sutton Piebald hogs on freshly tossed barley rusks in a newly-hosed byre.

Upon entering the office later the following morning, I saw Price gripping a printout of Svetlana's Tic Bird piece, holding it out before him like some Flying Scroll of Revelation. "I mean what the hell *is* this you've written here, Mensche?

"Listen to this: 'Once upon a time Charlie had a rock group, but they were all busted for drugs. Now he howls about his problems with freedom and affluence. He hates the Big Banks and consumerism, whose structure provides his free hand-outs from Social Security. He is also worried that his psychiatric social worker does not yet have his new iPod address.'"

I knew what was to come. I was the destroyer of the souls of the innocent.

"I mean can't you ever be nice to people, Mensche? What is all this scar tissue about, then? Can't you ever be sentimental, forgiving, caring?" God must have heard this, because Price's spoonful of *Celebrity Pork Roll* (in GM Quorn Macro-Brine) dropped to the floor, spattering a picture of Julie Burchill, making her appear as if she had a mouth full of pink froth.

Price cursed, screamed for a cleaner, gripped the Tic Bird *oeuvre* with damp hands, wiped his mouth on sleeve, and almost spat at me.

"I mean are you trying to *destroy* this man, Mensche?"

"Something like that."

"You can't *do* that these days! You can't be a journalist and destroy people!"

"Do you mind if I write that down?"

"And just hear this. I quote: 'Though Charlie just sits in a doorway, he gets a hundred quid a week from DSS to support his agony act plus a free subscription to a left-liberal newspaper where he will probably finish up as a sub-editor. As a bourgeois construct, Charlie's performance is truly *Anglais*.'"

"Who d'you think you're writing all this Carphone Warehouse stuff for, *The Guardian*? 'Bourgeois construct?' What the hell's that mean to plain honest *volk*? And you bet your life *Anglais* is a racist tag now, that's for sure. And what's this then? 'It cannot be said Charlie lacks determination. His suffering pout is now a celebrated postmodern signifier.' I mean what is one of them, for Christ's sake? And what's this, then? 'He is now a contender for the John Pilger Peasant's Saviour Award. He is now as British as the Three Day Week, Pork Scratchings, and Michael Parkinson's castration.' I mean can't you ever be merely *informative*, for a change? And what's this 'ere then? 'Like most actors, Charlie couldn't handle a garden hose without assistance, and his IQ is about sufficient to wipe his arse and lift a spoon to mouth. Ideal for a BBC3 Discursive Presenter.' Discursive? I'll have you know this is our Sunday edition for the *lumpen*. Are they going to understand such baboonage? Your take is positively anti-social."

"As soon as I hear the word 'social' I reach for my gun." The phrase was the Countess Svetlana's, not mine.

But I needn't have bothered. It went right over Price's head. "And listen to this: 'Charlie is heading for a top studio to have his croaks, squeaks, warbles and protests recorded. *Foxpig* has said he has *genre*. Those on the inside are already calling him pure retro-nursery-rhyme.'

I mean what's all that about, then? This is *The Brentford Sceptic*, not *Tesco's* finest pork-barrel supplement. And listen to this: 'Charlie is going to be mega. He's going to be the leading *agent provocateur* for the affluent *new lumpen*. The *Groucho* mob will love him. Soon he will take up his bed and walk. But don't hold your breath for loaves and fishes.' You've got this geezer all wrong, Mensche. He's a peasant, hug him like an old tree. His screams and his twanging banjo are taken as authentic working-class agony. Have you no respect?"

"I've done some research."

"God help us all."

"He's the alienated son of a Duke and Duchess."

"Now listen to me. I know he's a top nob. But if the punters learn he's a chinless wonder, all the stage fronts will collapse. Their dreams will disappear, their cocks will droop, and they won't work forty eight hours till they drop any more. That is why Charlie's got to stay disadvantaged, you get me?"

"Don't worry. His family's Welsh castle and two Elizabethan manor houses are well screened out."

"You're beginning to understand, Mensche. This is media — property, the past, all can be made invisible!"

This was new, I was intrigued. Was Price's old Communism slipping away? I had noticed recently that both his language and vocabulary were on the change. Fragment by fragment, the dialectic was dissolving like an old sock in a rotten rice pudding. Sooner or later I guessed that the *lumpen* idea would go. Like a fan in a gale, the internal dictionary pages were turning. Orwell's idea of the changing writing on the wall had nothing on this.

Price was downloading new software.

There had been rumours for some time in *The Ape* of a new woman in Price's life. According to Rabbit Finch, the biggest Press bullshitter between Brentford and Blackpool, Price had dropped into *The Ape* whilst I was on an assignment, to tell a fine new story. Apparently, overnight, Price's Communism had disappeared and he was quoted by Rabbit Finch as saying: "I want the *Sceptic* to become the *Evening Stand-*

ard of Brentford. Sex, WAGS, glamour, and ultra-smart ultra-smooth Amis, or whatever his name is. And film stars, that's what I want."

I didn't quite believe Rabbit at the time, but here was the evidence.

"I'm sorry, Price. A few old railway timetables are still inside me."

"You're getting old, Mensche. Charlie's a style leader. He's all software. Even *Gitmo* says he is the New Solution. It's a question of re-mythologise or die."

"I'd rather have a bucket of bran mash."

"Look you must realise that personality is just another product range. You can no more rage against it than dislike a lamppost. Detox yourself. You've got one foot in the grave, Mensche. If you're not careful, you'll go out with *Come Dancing*, and the Brentford Leisure Centre Martyrs of '73. Take a hint from me. I have deconstructed myself. It's like a whole-mind change. Get rid of the past. That's the secret."

Wonder of wonders — Communism had vanished in his head like an instantly forgettable commercial for Quorn pizza. Consumer time was running far faster than ever I thought.

"Now listen carefully. This is your big chance. I have got you an interview with Tony Blinge."

"The ex-Prime Minister?"

"The very same. You should be proud."

"Why me?"

"Because you have a good brand name. Sell it. You have got to think of product appeal. Your family played a big part in Scottish history."

"Where? We don't call it that."

"You're famous, d'you know that? Now just shut up and listen to me. Now Blinge went to school in Scotland."

"Where?"

"Shut up. He knew some of your famous family."

"The shame."

"Forget the cracks. This is our chance for Prime Time. Now listen carefully. One of your famous cousins who knows Blinge well personally got in touch with me early this morning and suggested that you interview the man himself. This could be big for *The Brentford Sceptic*, if only because of your famous name. I have fixed an interview already. By the way, Blinge has been reconstructed. He's found Jesus."

"That's one way of doing it."

Human beings were robots. Changing the programme was now the hi-tech metaphor for rebirth.

"It's all fixed. Get to *The Big Root Studios* first thing tomorrow morning."

four

A Disturbed Night
in Powis Square

I COULD hardly get out of this one. However, back at the Tabernacle, Betty came in useful. As an ex-Radio One DJ, she gave good Blinge.

"Greased pig of a boy scout. Difficult to catch. Talks in pure cliché. That smile will do well in Europe with the milk-maid commercials. Mental level low as a flooded underpass. Run by the Yanks. Key in his back they wind up occasionally. Dead white man. Long service socialist stripes on his arm. Honky *perfectus*. Don't let him smother you with parking fines or the rising cost of pillowcases. Get him on terrorism, immigration, paedophiles, Iraq, all the things he doesn't want to talk about."

With these thoughts in mind, I tried to sleep, but just after the witching hour, after my two nubiles had gorged themselves first upon myself, and subsequently upon one another, there came the sound of yet another catharsis erupting with the so-called problem family in ci-vilian accommodation next door.

The Pethers tribe leaguer on our left flank. Their numberless kith and kin are usually up all night making unlicensed shrink-wrapped sandwiches at a collective 75p per hour for equally unlicensed venues. This kind of work supports a local gipsy cottage industry throughout North Kensington.

The trouble started in fine style with Marla, Pethers' somewhat diffi-cult wife. On Benzine shots, E-tabs and Geralzipan, she started throw-ing the entire contents of the Pethers' household into the middle of the Talbot Road. Though Marla was from an old four-lavatory family in Dublin, Pethers had married beneath him. He was an Irish tinker. She was Irish. This night Marla surpassed herself. She accused Pethers (on permanent Tree-Frog, Lithium injections, and Prozac) and Flogger (Pethers' twenty three year old son, on bail and compulsory detoxification) and also Caroline, (Pethers' seventeen year old daughter, on permanent probation and compulsory analysis) of stealing her Methadone prescription.

All these whys and wherefores sallied out onto the pavement at precisely 00:00 hours, with the Plod soon arriving in lorry-loads, kitted out for another Normandy Invasion. Within minutes there was a Central Casting bomb-burst of legs, arms, very doubtful Ploughman's Lunches, and plenty of mixed tribal blood. The incantations of sins, debts, properties and favours of the Romany long-dead crashed onto the weedy tarmac. Claims and allegations both spiritual and temporal were made amidst discarded syringes, sodden Housing Benefit Refusal Letters, and torn and dilapidated demands for money from the Windsor family. Wafting aloft were severe warnings from many a Metropolitan Magistrate; warm commendations from Friends of the Earth; and secretly copied betrayals from the local collaborationist Neighbourhood Watch, whose addresses were well-marked by the Pethers' dynasty for any future day of reckoning and liberation.

I am a life-long collector and connoisseur of twentieth century written statements. To my great delight, I found amidst the Pethers' debris, a unique UNESCO grant application form. This I shall frame, complete with its decoration of *Mackson's Sausage-Paste*, yolk of suspicious egg, Ma Pethers' *Unique Pickle Oil*, and Jack Pethers' wondrous hand-scrawled claims for both charity and reality.

But I run ahead of my tale. Upon the stroke of 01:30, inspired by flashing blue lights, and the tyres screeching on what turned out to be gallons of rain-swept horseradish, I carefully disentangled myself from my paradisiacal nest of limitless female flesh, fur and form. I rolled my last twist of strong herbal shag, brewed a thimble of nettled water, and looked out, admiring the world as pure texture. Amidst marvellously disintegrated shards of not exactly the best convenience food technology, was such aggression, such overflowing life at long last free of both democracy and socialism — free, amidst the squashed mustard dispensers and stolen tumblers of *British Rail Surplus Mayonnaise* and, since Pethers has long since had his water cut off, free even of hygiene. Such life quite unlike mine! Life flowing free of intellect and sobriety! Life flowing free of conscious intelligence and its artificial complexities, even free of love, with its hurt and pain and eventual fall to corruption.

But as soldiers say (I wish I had the courage to be one), morale is always lowest before dawn. Head bowed, I turned from my window, I was fallen from the Pethers universe, with my endless articulation, the broken compass of my intelligence, and the last diseased remnants of my over-educated reason.

How I pity Pethers. Yum Yum: just wait till the Caring Folk get their loving game-show hands on his particular spectacular array of good-cause delicacies. Compassionate hands will wipe Pethers' arse faster than he can curse, and for a tinker that is fast. First thing the Loving Ones will do is get rid of the useful family sandwich business, and give the Pethers family the designer-drug of new keyboard opportunities, plus a free license-voucher to get tucked up some sausage-jockey's arse before *Book at Bedtime*. Now, there's a clever one from the well-meaning! No bombs, needles, no Orwellian rats nibbling at Pethers' old gipsy skull, not even a single psychiatric social worker in sight, hauled squealing from her dedicated Ladbroke Grove peasant commitments.

"Relax, Pethers," I remember saying to myself, "Calm down and give thanks for thy rescue, just look at the coloured lights as the grant-aided ones, like descending aliens, move towards thee. Stay thou flooded by hypnotic lights of the democratic experience," said I, "And wait for thy coming lobotomy with the resignation of the early saints."

Some devilish seed in me makes me very grateful for these disturbed nights of the early twenty-first-century cosmos, if only because they prevent me from relaxing. I hate being calm. Can't help seeing the damage it always does. Any peace and tranquillity stops me asking questions. Even now, I ask the question — what is brain? How about that? What a thing to ask before breakfast in a difficult week, which began seven days ago, with a Benefit cancellation delivered in the name of the

Guardian of North European Protestant Mysteries, and further rejections of my wives' masterpieces from the wine bar Fionas and bangled Jeremys of no less than sixty-five publishers?

Was I born for such realism, I say?

What is mind? And what is waste?

There I go again.

five

The Blinge Doctrine of Nature

I DISEMBARKED at Camden Town utterly exhausted from the Pethers' frolics. A black polluted sky hung over the entrance to that modern Hades called *The Big Root Television Studio*. It was one of those English May mornings that poets don't write about: by the time of what *The Evening Standard* called "Early Roll Call for the City Slaves," London had experienced three full-size motorway pile-ups and two deaths through road rage. In addition to these City woes, a sudden downpour drowned a toddler in his pram outside an *Asda* store whilst security guards frisked his mother. Eventually staff found a purloined copy of the *TV Times* stuffed in her tights.

The great man himself was all over me; I was famous family, **ancien** royalty, and all that. But Betty was right about him being a greased pig. Blinge was a somewhat tricky boy, to say the least; I managed the interview as best I could, and got the DVD to Price by courier. I spent the rest of the day in bed recovering from the experience.

Late morning, next day. The office of the *Sceptic*. Trouble loomed large on the brick-laying brow of Price as he pointed to a large screen showing Blinge's famous *Basil Brush* smile in all its glory.

"Mensche, what the hell is this then?"

"What is what?"

"Sit down."

Price clicked his remote. I came on screen, talking to Blinge.

"Mr. Blinge, some say you've got a big problem here with bomber suspects. They keep escaping abroad, and the ones you catch are freed long before they serve their sentence."

"Now don't be sexist."

"Sexist?"

"There are women involved as well. So don't be judgmental."

"Well, what about the old lags? 2,000 went free on Friday."

"There were women amongst those, too. 2,000, did you say? That's not many for our population."

"And there's 10,000 Polish thespian poofs arriving on Saturday. If they come, by Sunday night there won't be a child bride left in the whole of the *Groucho Club*."

Price got up and clicked the remote. The screen froze. Blinge's famous grin became a hare hung up in a butcher's shop. Price turned to me, his face boiling with anger.

"Mensche, who the hell do you think you are? How can we publish this stuff, never mind sell it to the Broadcasters? You're pushing him with jokes he'll never understand in a month of Sundays. His current act is still Mr. Super Simple Suburbia, remember? He can't admit to knowing what the *Groucho* is. We will have to do this whole thing over again. You should have smiled at him, praised him. You should have asked him about painting the garage, car parking problems and tax on washing machines. Remember it's only filing clerks with mortgages who will be watching this stuff in any case. We can't use all this abrasive rude so-called meaningful stuff of yours. Did you see the poor bugger? You made him nervous. You don't talk to a Prime Minister about politics, for Christ's sake!"

"Wait. The rest of it is superb."

Price screamed down the outer corridor.

"Somebody run out and get me a Mars Bar! I'm dying in here."

"Patience, Price. Listen to this."

Blinge continued, rallying a little with his famous foxy smile.

"You see, everybody has to be supplied. Everything we think about is a question of supply and demand. Media's like any other supermart, bring yourself up to date."

"Everyone suggests I do that."

"The Polish recession heroes you sneer at are essential cultural supplies, now. They're Tutti-Frutti or Mandelson Treacle and Honey Bars.

Run out of dolly-men and poofs, and your TV screen would be a blank. Jesus, cut that last bit, will you? Ahem. And then where would we be? Oh by the way, you've got to read this book *The Rumford Rogues*, by Dr. Deborah Rumford, one of my wife's favourite authors. At first I thought it was going to be pure New Age baboonage, you know, one of those cure-your-cat's-farting-overnight kinds of crappola that cons millions very quickly. This book is different: it will digitise you, make you swing again like you did last summer."

I remember my heart jumped at the time. For a few seconds I thought he was going to try and do *The Twist*.

"All the Corrie and Ender fruitcakes have got it. It's great for Flatlanders. Lifts you right out of it."

Aha! He'd used the word "Flatlanders," my mother's term for all Britannic unfortunates. Quite amazing how these things travelled and developed!

"Mr Blinge, according to *The Sun*, there's another 24,000 dangerous scallywags being freed this year on Remand."

"They will *not* be free. They've been told to report to a police station every day. Do you call that being free?"

"Most of them don't turn up at any police station. Many are not British citizens, decent or otherwise."

"Give them time."

"For what?"

"To adjust."

"To what?"

"Social democracy. You see you absolutely must realise that almost all of these people are rock-rough peasants. Oh God, cut that will you?"

"Now sir, may I have your opinion on this editorial from *The Sun*?"

"Certainly."

"'As many as 1,200 drug dealers, burglars and fraudsters will be freed early from prison today — to combat an overcrowding crisis. Releasing these criminals will be one of the first acts of the new government, although the plans were set out two weeks ago. The move to free non-dangerous offenders up to eighteen days early means 25,000 prisoners will be let out of jail early over the course of a year.' Now Mr. Blinge, is this a good idea?"

"Absolutely."

"With what object?"

"Rehabilitation."

"What does that mean?"

"We let them go free."

"That's brilliant."

"Yes, it's that simple. No incarceration. With rehabilitation, you don't have to put anybody anywhere. Good idea, yes?"

"So there's no need to keep them in jail?"

"Exactly."

"That's brilliant again."

"Thank you. You see with the — er — working class — Oh God, cut again, will you —"

Price clicked pause, bit a fingernail, and gave me a long look.

"We can't use this. Even with cuts and re-editing, we can't use it."

"Have patience."

"I wish I'd never left Retail."

"Rejoice."

"What are we going to do?"

"You are seeing the birth of a new *genre*."

"Genre? It was tat like this ruined *Bric-a-Brac*."

Reluctantly, Price clicked his remote. Blinge continued.

"These New Citizens — Oh God, am I fucking up tonight. Don't worry. Just a touch of Work Load. How'd you feel if you'd just spent the afternoon with a convention of Social-Democratic Left-Liberal Railing-Painters for the Socialist New Century?"

"Not good, but let me ask you another thing. Now why are you letting all these foreigners into Britain?"

"Because they need us."

"There's another remarkable thought, sir!"

"Remarkable bollocks!" Price howled, pointing his remote in dismissal, but I snatched it away.

"Have patience, Price. Buy Blinge's new book, *Look, Listen, and Learn.*"

"God help me."

I reactivated Blinge. A cough, a sip of water. He straightened up and resumed with his best public address accent.

"You see, once here, these New Citizens have options they don't have in their own countries. Give them time. In a social democracy, it's their choice. You see with the — er — working class — er — Oh God, cut again, will you? You must realise, the people you're referring to are probably off somewhere taking proper advice from their social workers and legal representatives. Could be a variety of reasons for their non-appearance. Could be problems with their sexuality. They've somehow become terribly confused about this, and they've panicked. Their option of taking sexual advice is their decision as part of their implicit social contract. It's the people's choice. If you ask me, you're judging them before the event. It's all about choice. They may have worries about applying for citizenship, hence their aggression. They may have an AIDS problem. We must make things easier for them. It's all about caring, no matter what happens. Even if they decide to fight our Law, it's alright by me, I'm a democrat. Maybe nervous social workers gave them advice in fundamental conflict with Binding Statutes. This will require all kinds of rearrangements, by Team Leaders of the social workers, and the Team Leader' community legal advisors (many of whom belong to my party) may well work out an alternative procedural path for the Afro-English to follow."

"The who?"

"Afro-English. I have an Afro-English friend."

"From which country?"

Blinge looked flustered as he gave the celebrated Sarah Palin reply.

"Africa."

"Oh."

"Don't be embarrassed. You can call them call New Citizens. if you like"

"That's a bit better."

"You see I'm all for Organised Advice by Professional Care. That's the framework of social-democratic mortality, I mean morality."

"No Stop and Question?"

"I beg your pardon? Oh no, certainly not, would *you* like to be stopped and questioned? As possible British citizens who do not speak good English, they may be both confused and fearful. They might panic, they'd forget to go to the Job Centre on the right date, and their whole support system will collapse, and the social workers will have to clear up the whole mess. A lost signing day just is not funny. Their Benefit won't arrive. And if you are watching this interview in hiding, I do hope you realise that. They may also lose their counselling for depression, alcoholism or homosexual problems. You see with these black folk — oh shit, cut again!"

"Why do criminals get full Social Security?"

"Really, you must not call them criminals. That so depends on circumstances. Not to worry. Whenever such people choose to come out of hiding, the social workers will give proper advice and legal representation."

"What if one of their bombs goes off by accident and kills several social workers?"

"Well of course, that would be most unfortunate. But the social workers would, of course, be fully insured professionally, and my sympathy would go to their family — and not forgetting the families of the bombers. Fair dues. Reality is a matter of fairness, democracy and civil liberties. Everything is a matter of civil liberties."

"Do bombers care about civil liberties?"

"Well, they might eventually. Some, I admit, are being very silly. And that admittedly bad behaviour must stop,"

"You think these terrorist suspects will take advice?"

"I'm glad you used the word *suspects*."

"Some of the suspects have disappeared. I'd say it's suspicious that they did not report, wouldn't you?"

"Don't jump to conclusions. They may yet report to their Support Groups. Support Groups are reality as far as I am concerned. We have to support anything and everything. That's the name of the game. Support is the new secular religion."

Of a sudden, to Price's pop-eyed astonishment, Blinge stood up straight like some scroll-reading madman on Mount Sinai, screaming out loud.

"Come to me, all you withered fuck-ups and disasters! I will wash thee, kiss thy feet in the name of Faith, Hope, Charity, and that new angel called Support!"

"Now Mr. Blinge, please get hold of yourself."

He sat down, sweating and exhausted. So did Price.

"I'm sorry. It's the passion. Just passion and all-consuming socialist commitment to vast hosts of the fallen. These — er — lost foreign — er — what did I say?"

"New Citizens."

"Thank you. They may have gone to reclaim a miscalculated Benefit, and that takes time."

"Do the police check these cases?"

"Police? This is a matter for social workers, not the police. Such individuals may have been thrown out of their DSS hostel for any reason at all, and that's a serious matter. They may not have anywhere to lay their heads, have you ever thought about that?"

"If they're found, will they be questioned?"

"By whom?"

"The police."

"You keep talking about the police. I've made sure the police can't stop and question anybody. It's now illegal."

"But these New Citizens of yours might be preparing another bomb somewhere."

"That's a separate issue."

"Will the social workers question them?"

"Oh yes. It's very important to realise that."

"And they will pass on the information to the police?"

"Only when it's relevant."

"Like possession of explosives and detonators?"

"Look, let's get our priorities right. First the social workers will want to know whether these — er — New Britons, yes?"

"That's better."

" — and Middle-Easterners —"

"That's terrible. Try again."

"Shiites."

"No, no."

"New Citizens."

"Do at a pinch."

"Afro-British? Nelson Mandela?"

"Mr. Blinge, please get a grip."

"Oh God, I've corpsed. What the hell is wrong with me today?"

"Try colonials, or something like that."

"The black colonials?"

Price seized the remote. The screen froze once more.

"This is terrible. I've seen part-time Hosiery Managers do better than this."

"Wait. It gets better."

"I'm glad to hear that. At this rate we won't make Radio Four early Sunday morning. Mensche, do you ever LIKE anything or anyone at all?"

"Only junk. I collect it. It's art form. And Blinge is the best piece of dumped clockwork since Maggie Thatcher. Enjoy!"

"Oh God, I wish I was back in Knitwear!"

"Watch this next bit and you'll never look back."

"We're ruined."

"Not quite just yet. Listen to this."

Blinge came back in full flight.

"First the social workers will want to know whether these New Visitors, oh shit. Cut, please."

"Try, immigrants."

"Okay. Ahem. The question of whether these immigrants are gay or lesbian is of vital importance to what is called profiling for any related disabilities. You see this awful bombing impulse is often a function of tensions within these categories. It is of far more importance to know where these people are within the Human Needs Spectrum. Any proper socio-political analysis starts from there."

"Many are in hiding. What happens if they are found?"

"They will just have to re-register with the appropriate agencies. They will have to go through the DSS paperwork again. The social workers will help them through the fresh documentation, see if any have Special Needs within the, say, the Drugs Rehabilitation programme."

"Supposing they detonate more bombs?"

"You're making assumptions. Many of the people you are talking about are first-generation DSS applicants. Their behaviour may lead to certain difficulties, I agree, but you've got to realise that losers from failed states matter. Oh God, cut that, will you? You've got to remember that we are not dealing here with people who will sit by the fire and read *The Radio Times*. That would be an ideal solution, but these coloured folk are all very excitable. That's why they're good at music and dance, and all that kind of caper. Oh God, cut that will you? Now let's get back to talking about what caring is all about. Everybody has care-oriented needs. And losers most of all. Cut that please. You see it's all about social-scientific democracy. Even terrorists have needs. The bottom matters as much as does the top. It's all about information. They may not be aware of homosexual housing projects for example, or the new experimental Free Clean Needle Programmes now available all over the country."

"Hallelujah."

"I beg your pardon?"

"Sorry, sir. I was overwhelmed there for a moment."

"The pace of modern information flow does that to me too, on occasion. I keep taking some soft options myself, stops me getting overwhelmed."

"What soft options are those?"

"The Liberal Arts. A good daily dose of the gender-neutral English Liberal Arts keeps your mental anus as clean as Carol Vorderman's TV kitchen top, dear boy."

Price, aghast, seized the remote and froze Blinge's face into a wartime poster of *Careless Talk Costs Lives*.

"Did he just *say* that, did he actually say that?"

"Don't worry. We can dump the off-cuts on YouTube."

Grabbing back the remote I unfroze Blinge's face from wartime effigy.

"Pastel shades, that's what these bombers need. Their inner landscape is too high-energy. Too many peaks and troughs. English expression will cure that. The ethnic novelists have shown what even pseudo-Englishness can do to calm a troubled soul. Not even the IRA could stand up to English pastel shades. The Muslims don't stand a chance. They'll all be eating salmon and cress sandwiches in Bath and reading Evelyn Waugh before they know it."

Price hit the remote again. Blinge's face now hung up like a discoloured giraffe-loin chop in an abandoned Congolese eat-in.

"Why didn't you ask the poor fellow something about Jesus, for Christ's sake?"

"I don't know anything about Jesus. I'd rather worship the sacred temple monkeys of Grand Bassin."

"Well you should have improvised! Everybody else does!"

"I didn't have a nightshirt and a pair of sandals handy, did I?"

"Now listen, Mensche. I've just about had enough of these clever-clever *bon mots* of yours. They're soiled goods. Why don't you do yourself a favour and do a stock take of your brain? Find out the profits and the losses and all that. Do you a power of good."

"I've told you. It gets better."

"Better? What does that mean?"

"Listen. It all makes sense after a while."

"God help us!"

I clicked again. Blinge's face came back on screen like a nodding skeleton in the back window of a hearse.

"Now remember the bombers are casualties too, in a way. If and when they are found, they will need money, clothing, food and accommodation just like anyone else. You simply have to care about caring. You like that phrase? I'm having it made into a lapel badge for the Party Conference."

"Will the caring be launched before or after a bombing?"

"It doesn't matter. Caring is *caring*. There's no limit to it. Even bombers are human beings. They can have what the social workers call Special Needs Green Counselling, for example. Then there's the *other* Green manifesto relating to changes in the evolving pattern of parking-fine regulations …"

Blinge was now rubbing his eyes and staring into space. I had to help him out.

"No, no, Mr. Blinge. Wrong fairy tale. Wrong script."

"Gay working class. Yes?"

"We've done that one."

"Give me a cue."

"We were talking about the terrorists who have escaped recently."

He woke up. Circuit boards slipped into the connectors. Power was switched back on. The formulas came back on screen.

"Oh yes. Gender frustration could give us a clue to their actions."

"And the people on the pavement with their legs blown off?"

"I can't see the point of that question. Such are hardly in a position to prove anything, are they? I mean, what do they know at that time? They'll accuse anybody of anything. It's a favourite target, of course, people of Arab appearance. How do the wounded whites know that what has happened is a political act?"

"Can I quote you on that?"

"You have got to weigh things in the balance."

"What about the dead?"

"Well you know I've always said that it's prudent to arrange comprehensive family Insurance."

"So within the super-caring dimension you say the terrorists also suffer?"

"Yes, they may be suffering as well, and we've got to be fair to them just as we are fair to the victims. Remember, Christ suffered as did they."

"Was there ever anyone who *didn't* suffer?"

"What? No, that's not possible. Suffering is what it's all about. That's why I am a Christian. Let's get this straight. The only thing you can do is somehow alleviate suffering. In hospital or prison, all parties can get advice from psychiatric social workers. Got to be fair. That's what it's all about. Whether gay or straight, silly or sensible, we will rush to their side. Yes, that's democracy for all these Cape coloured worthy oriental wooftahs ... whirling Watsui ... Oh God, I'm so sorry. Work load, that's what it is. Just work load."

Price leaped to the remote and Blinge's face froze once more, suspended in Flatland time like a sepia shot from a *Keystone Cops* film. "Mensche, why is it we can never ever use a single piece of yours? I send you out to interview an ex-Prime Minster and all you get from him is this whirling Watsui and the terrorist need for gay counselling."

"We can sell the good bits to the French."

"We couldn't sell this to the baby-farmers of Madagascar. It was never like this in Hosiery. Only you could do this to people. Have you ever heard of houses and gardens and children and puppies? I mean, what about holidays, favourite foods and TV programmes?"

"Wait. The next bit's more authentic."

Blinge's face came out of freeze-frame like cannibal meat from an unpowered fridge.

"What about the families of the terrorists, Prime Minister?"

"As long as they do not lose Benefit, they will be alright. I do admit that if the explosion occurs on a signing-on day at the labour exchange, it complicates things. They may be in sheltered housing or in a bed and breakfast hostel. Rest assured, the social workers will make all the proper social-democratic arrangements for the victims, of whatever sexual persuasion. You have to bear in mind that in most cases the bombers are victims, too."

"Of what?"

"Bad housing, for example, and poor communication, and lack of popular social support. And racism. Victimisation at work and play. Gender sexism, homophobia. All people suffer from such things, and so-called terrorists are no exception. They may need crisis management."

"How can people help in this situation?"

"Talk to potential terrorists. Seek them out in their classrooms, coffee houses and Internet cafes. Ask them if they need bank loans, or have Methadone supply problems. Try to understand just what has produced the bombing situation. Tell them psychiatric social workers are there to be used."

"Thank you. Well Prime Minister, what do you think is the solution?"

"More imams."

"More what?"

"More Imams mean that the — er — Commonwealth — er — black — er — New Citizens are welcome — no, no, that's not right. The Colonial — er — Empire-Chinese mixed-race, oh bollocks. South of Calais. Oh shit. What's the bloody name for them? It's gone right out of my top-knot. Cut that."

The component boards controlling names and myths had short-circuited again. Robot bio-engineers inside his skull were dashing around replacing them. It took all of ten seconds after my prompt.

"Try Muslims."

"What? No. Oh yes. Muslims in the main. And don't forget we all need commitment to bringing about intense re-socialisation of the Muslim culture, gay or straight, rich or poor, alcoholic or DSS Needs Dependent. We must try to get at the root of the problem. These poor ex-slaves. Cut that. Disadvantaged peasantry, whatever. Everybody needs the DSS solutions-culture, which is there to provide designer-answers in the multicultural world."

"Thank you, Mr. Blinge."

"Thank you for sharing your needs. Take Advice from the Centres that are there for your convenience. Always. Keep on sharing and caring with the New Citizen community."

"Mr. Blinge, if you don't mind, a private question off the record."

"Go ahead."

"Do you really care?"

"Not really. Caring has nearly ruined my life. I'm going home now to see a new CD version of *Triumph of the Will*. Does wonders for your sex life. Barbara and myself always screw to this film, and there's a new digitised enhanced version."

Just for a moment, the *Basil Brush* smile came back.

"But don't let the Pope know."

Price switched off the screen, and flung the remote through the open window, where it landed with a clang on a clutch of dustbins below.

"You have wasted the £255 I spent on this project!"

"We can create something here. This is Reality TV Proper. Better than some pathetic attempt at profundity. Better than Jade, even."

"Now don't you speak ill of the gods."

"Call it *The Junk Cosmos*. The punters will love it. Did you see all that baboonage in action? It's a masterpiece! And don't laugh."

"I am not laughing. I am thinking about the money I've lost."

"You lost a lot more in Hosiery."

"Only fifty quid more. Now listen to me carefully. Get in here early tomorrow morning. Something big is in the wind. You'll have to go to Nottingham and interview this punk-child who's got the rock universe by the knackers at the moment."

"What's her name?"

"Names don't really matter anymore in the stellar regions, boy. I think sometimes she's called Portcullis Maid Marian. You'll love her. She'll get you up to date, and she's only ten."

"Bit old for you, isn't she?"

"Proud of these tactics, are you, Mensche?"

"Can't help it. I have a criminal nature. I don't want to be socialised."

Much laughter from down the corridor. Price put his glowering head out the door and screamed at the nether regions of *The Brentford Sceptic*. "Ah, shut up, this man is going to save us."

Laughter again. I had a feeling that they obviously knew something I did not.

Price turned to me with twinkling eyes. This meant that he was again delighted to steer me into trouble. He raised his voice once more.

"And don't fuck this one up, Mensche! I want trendy sex, glamour and rock'n'roll."

"I'm your man."

Again, cat-calls and hoots of derision from the inner regions of *The Sceptic*. God must have listening to the general mirth, because an open tin of *Celebrity Pork Roll* decided in its wisdom to jump off Price's desk of its own accord. It bounced off his bare sandaled toes, and spread oozing pink goo all over a *TV Times* picture of Julian Clary.

My last vision of the day was Price trying to organise mops and buckets, surrounded by a giggling and reluctant staff.

I left the office with foreboding.

six

Maid Marian in Distress

THE NEXT day, immediately upon arriving in Nottingham, I did not have long to wait to see what Price had been talking about. A crowd of obviously star-fucked worshippers blocked Main Street. At the centre of their attention was a stalled stretch limo, with the heads of two RAC engineers deep inside the bonnet. There emerged from the black-windowed vehicle a sneering child with a mass of white-bleached hair towering above wraparound dark glasses.

No more than ten years of age, she was followed by an entourage of four massive black bodyguards, a fussing hairdresser, a prancing butler, and an overweight sullen female companion who shouted orders to all and sundry like a sergeant major on parade. Every single one of these *personae* jabbered into a mobile and wore identical dark glasses. A dwarf emerged carrying a V-shape *Fender* guitar, which he wielded like an M-16. A chimpanzee in a red skirt wearing earmuffs under a *fez*, helped unload a set of speakers.

There couldn't possibly be more than one such manifestation in one city — inadvertently, I'd come across the object of my journey. The screams and chants alone told me this child was indeed Portcullis Maid Marian, now (to roars of appreciation) stamping her tiny foot, and roundly cursing the sweating RAC engineers.

Though her naked chest was flat as a draining board she sported a skilfully sprayed-on black bra, and a thong that would have got her arrested a year previous (which was a long time ago in pubic time).

As if straight from a hot porn shot, she licked a pink two-headed ice cream handed to her from a refrigerated hamper carried by the prancing butler. How her eyes rolled in appreciation as she gazed at a a nearby hoarding of a glamorous woman television personality licking an identical piece of cartoon-bait. I was indeed impressed: here were two Disney chipmunk-faces in cartoon symbiosis, both saying *eat more* until the information balloon from one became identical to the cream-smeared lips of the other. The commercials of the living and the dead said the same thing: *gorge till you become Queen of all things!*

All acts of occultism scare me. But if, (as some claimed), she was the Anti-Christ, then I was disappointed. I didn't know the Devil was so hard up. Usually he had a whiff of raw-boned evil about him. But perhaps, getting lost in the sale queues I could see everywhere in Nottingham, perhaps even Satan had lost his touch, gone to a damp stain on a viewing settee, and the cartoon maze had interviewed him to death. Yes, here in Nottingham, Queen of the Flatlands, poor old metaphysical Evil had been pasteurised! A nice end for the Devil, destroyed by his own creation. John Milton would be most pleased.

Something warned me not to look at the scene direct. Certainly it was brilliantly intense. The little Queen waved, gesticulated and screamed rap-babble to clashing chords played by the amp-hobbled dwarf. Turning my back on her, therefore, I fixed my attention on her gesticulating reflection in the plate glass of a shop window. Low-light dilution is such a wonderful thing, it demystifies the high-contrast symbols within the advertising structure of such scenes. Only partially irradiated by these hunting rapacious images, I felt like those fortunate few who happened to be behind a lead screen in a hospital X-ray room when the first atomic bomb was dropped on Hiroshima. (But then, I never fall ill, why? I always assume it's because I did not *consume*. I mentally excreted all input, *Tellytubbies*, *News at Ten*, all went The Way of the Water Closet, the sand tray, and my spewing mouth.)

Serious thoughts. My editor would not like them.

Crash and howl — I looked back. Always a bad thing to do.

The ten year old Queen, apparently now in a kind of sudden tantrum, snatched the dwarf's *Fender*, and threw both her ice cream and the instrument to the middle of the road, where both were promptly flattened by a passing hearse, of all things. She screamed obscenities at every single one of her entourage until the reserve limo arrived. Finally, she collapsed into the rescue vehicle like a mini-Garbo in distress.

Men, women, children, pensioners, dogs, now dived to the surface of the road, where they licked streams of ice cream off the splinters of smashed *Fender*, as if they were pieces of a True Cross. The kids licked broken shards of the lollipop relic, the men sucked blood from their scratched fingers. Kids howled, dogs peed, the women fought, and the second limo stalled, the driver revving the engine furiously.

A white oval face in the back window gazed at the crowd as they seethed around the cab, screaming, *Portcullis Maid Marian!*

Fingers scraped the windows, and she screamed and laughed to urge them on. The driver revved, the engine started and the goddess Portcullis escaped, some worthies trailing from the back mudguard. One overweight male fan slipped off the roof of the limo into the gutter with a sickening thump.

He rolled over, then stood up and danced on the spot as if he were quite mad. Another miracle from Portcullis Maid Marian! The crowd roared!

I caught the thinnest of smiles in the thinnest of shadows as the ten-year-old raced to her illimitable rendezvous in her speeding chariot. A tiny hand waved. Jesus, she'd noticed me thinking. A last wave. You are finished, says she. I am going to win, thinks she.

A thought. The superchild Portcullis was telling me what had happened. Like thinking indeed, suffering had gone in turn, Suffering, like reading and writing, had crept out like a thief in the night. Billions of happy-jack screens fed Portcullis's manic iPod-eaters till they were junked up with things they could never have, horizons they would never see. Already her fans in particular could hardly tell the difference between the living, the dead or the mad.

Happiness was here.

Suffering had been deconstructed.

I saw their glazed eyes looking for the most minute fragments of the smashed *Fender*. Within a short stretch of media time this exhalted banjo would become holy history, seeding other dreams in other parts of the city, and indeed the galaxies.

Breathless, thirsty, and somewhat terrified, I struck out for the famous Trip to Jerusalem, the oldest hostelry in the Flatlands. Draining a pint of the local brew from the wood, I sat and wondered what had been in the heads of the crusading soldiery who once sat in my place and thought of fighting their way to Jerusalem.

Was Portcullis historical success? Was she the Next Stage? Was she the final dream of the visionaries and mechanists, did she represent the social-scientific dream of something called "improvement" of the human condition? A tart looking ten years older than her ten years, already world-weary, but moving forward all history with the ease of Atlas with the world on his shoulders. All intellect quite defeated. Only people with brains had the problems: searching for order, merit and their beloved meaningful harmonies, they grew stiff and their own rigidity broke them up. No, the Weights and Measures folk with their Rules and Regulations universe were not going to last long in Portcullis Time.

Ten year old Portcullis, with thong up her pre-pubic muff and arse, was universal boneless and brainless flexibility, adaptable to the life and death of many species, gut and memory. This Queen and her universal brood had changed the galaxies back into the spew of the gods. Her kind, conjured up all over the world at the same time, would breed the next generations of heroes: thin, brainless, slumped in club doorways with their smashed guitars, needles sticking out of their brainless arms. An equally brainless anorexic supermodel would be their angel of death, screaming for police, lawyers and photographers.

Portcullis Maid Marian was the perfect junk-cosmology. Her vacuity was going to win the Darwinian race.

Who or what begat her? I suspected her parents became victims of spontaneous combustion soon after she bridled at the teat.

Meantime, before annihilation, I could hear the superchild's brothers and sisters banging and twanging their ukuleles and banjos in every bar and bistro and boutique as if there were no tomorrow — and for them there probably was no tomorrow, for not one of them was built to last in the old sense. Transient as the multi-coloured pastes and powders that stuffed their gills, their world was a temporary bit of scaffolding in an almost no Time at all. In a way, these countless minstrels were the last Human Beings. Few would get past eighteen years of age before being dead or mad. And they all knew this, of course. Like the mini-Garbo, they were built for consumer annihilation like a moth, greenfly, or *Celebrity Pork Roll*. Meantime, before the End (which was nigh) their screams, sorrows and loves shot out of every screen and speaker. Their warbles and shouts were fit for the dog-howling of all history. If the West had a death rattle, it was the screams of these singing infants.

Mobile tones. Price. He changed them every day. The Pearl Harbor Speech. Elvis Presley in the background.

*Yesterday, December 7*th*, 1941 — a date which will live in infamy — the United States of America was suddenly and deliberately attacked by naval and air forces of the Empire of Japan.*

"Having a nice day then, Mensche?"

"I don't have them. I am not a nice person."

"Well fake it for me, then. Just once. Done any interviews yet?"

"There's nobody here. They've uploaded. All of 'em. Families, furniture, food, everything, all uploaded. You should try it sometime. That way, you don't miss a minute of every single channel, and there's no license fee. This is the first uploaded town. And its all free. They don't need sets any longer. They all got through the pain barrier when they went online without a terminal."

"Nobody will understand this."

"This is pure TV. This Upload Zone MK1. Understanding anything at all is not required. This is the Prime Time town. The Stepford Wives have nothing on this —"

"And what is a Prime Time town?"

"Non-cerebral system."

"You come out with some good phrases, boy. Your last headline *When I Fantasise I Investigate* cost us 10,000 readers in Greater Brentford alone."

"Was that figure arrived at before we junked the entire run, or after?"

"Your famous remarks got reported by *The Guardian*, but that's not a good sign for a peasant paper like *The Brentford Sceptic*. If we do any more of that A&F stuff as you call it, we'll be watching French films, eating Quorn quiche, and being nice to homos. Let's face it, the peasants don't like all that South-of-Calais bollocks of yours. That's best left to the Jews and the Germans and look what thinking did for them. You done anything yet on Portcullis Maid Marian?"

"It's difficult. She's got a lawyer, a manager, an agent, and apparently she screws emaciated rock-yokels by the tumbril load."

"Which means that she'll get round to you eventually."

"I'd rather have a Barnyard enema on All Souls' Night."

"I admit she's a bit risky for Brentford, but we've all got to move on. You should do exactly that. Get a fantasy life. Facts went out when they scrapped the old Vanguard battleship in 1946. But perhaps you shouldn't be doing this at your age. Perhaps I should not let an ancient ratbag like you anywhere near a ten year old young nymphette."

"She's much too old for me. My genes don't go back that far."

"They won't understand all this in Brentford. Can you interview this young cow and do something useful before I sack you?"

"You'd like it here. There's plenty of inland sailors at *The Salutation*, or so I've been told. I'll send your wife the address to keep for you."

"Well get me some sensible copy soon, that's all I can say. And keep off the nymphette, for Christ's sake. Ciao for now. Power to the people!"

But Portcullis Maid Marian was still in my head. Had I found the genie of the place? Did all manner of things here radiate from her? Was she what all the old ballroom scenes had shrunk to?

I went to the local seed shop, where it was said they knew everything. I asked about Portcullis. Mr. and Mrs. Bentley enthused, alternating like figures from a cuckoo clock.

"She lives in the old Palais de Danse. She bought it years ago."

"She's made millions."

"They say it's haunted. Ghost of somebody called Gene Mayo, a Mecca dance band leader from the days of formation dancing."

"You won't get in there. She's surrounded by police and fans all day."

"And prowling psychopaths at night. They reckon she's got ex-Special Forces teams looking after her. They've all gone mad about her here, expecially the fuits and nuts. One poured petrol over himself only last week and burned himself alive because she refused him what she calls an audience."

"Another bloke threw himself off Trent Bridge the week before."

"All over her."

"Whilst she's on stage she's safe. But every lunatic in the world is waiting. They've tried everything: shooting and knife attacks, bombs, gas —"

Mrs Bentley's voice dropped to a whisper.

"She's an old fairy queen, that's why. Some reckon she's a healer."

I stopped taking notes. Mrs. Bentley did appear to be the kind of person to talk about queens, fairies or healers, or otherwise.

"A fairy queen?"

"Portcullis is bit of old pantomime. That's all it needs, can't say any more. It's old, you understand."

"I understand."

Feeling a bit peckish, I bought two packets of *Hartley's Maize Chews* with NOT FOR PREGNANT SOWS written on the back. Not the best dining perhaps, but anything was better than *les anglais* "Pork Scratchings" which I saw young children buying from a counter to my right. A couple of hours of TV in the gut as well as the pork scratchings I supposed would guarantee that someone somewhere would buy a rifle, enter a supermarket, and start shooting at people as if they were labels on tins.

Mrs. Bentley smiled as she gave me my change.

"Do you mind if I ask you a personal question?"

"No, not at all."

"Where have you parked your spaceship?""

Laughter all round.

"Madam: would you ask that of Christ on the Cross?"

In the ensuing deadly silence I took my leave and headed for the old *Palais de Dance*.

seven

Interviewing the Anti-Christ

MOVING PAST queues of penitents and patients screaming for healing, I presented my *Brentford Sceptic* credentials to a bouncer who put me before a screen in the foyer of the old dance hall. The face of Portcullis appeared.

"Oh, it's YOU."

Amazing what she could do with a glimpse from the back of her car.

"Good morning."

"Oh, very 1940s. Who the fuck are you?"

"My name is George Mensche. I'd like to interview you for *The Brentford Sceptic*."

"You want to audition?"

"Does it look like it?"

"Well what's a decrepit fart like you want with me? My pussy is for young movers, not memories of the Spanish Armada."

"I'm not after your pussy."

"Christ, a miracle. Everybody else is. How old are you, Fuzzball?"

"92,000 years, madam."

"Where'd you get that figure from, boy?"

"The Great Pyramid of Giza, madam."

"You'll soon be dead."

"Good. You can count."

"And you'll feel a lot better for it."

"Dead?"

"That's right. The sooner the better. John, let this perished jockstrap in. Looks as if he's in need of a good kicking."

Two bouncers frisked me. I was told not to come within five feet of Portcullis, and not to make any quick movements in front of her. They led me to a drawbridge over a flowing stream. Quite impressive, and it all came with the scent of armpits and opium, the smell of a good-class Turkish brothel at the end of the old Empire. There were no visible walls, only drapes blown by a wind machine. The floor was a masterpiece. It must have been built on some kind of rotating arm beneath, because it changed its angles randomly from nought to about ten degrees, then tipped again from another of its hexagonal sides. Portcullis Maid Marian sat on a transparent throne in the Egyptian style. Because of the rolling floor, supplicants such as I were made to approach like a sailor on deck in a gale.

Henry, the biggest black man I have ever seen in my life, sat on a stool in a corner watching me as he rolled joints and distributed opium pipes to at least a dozen young bodies strewn around, some with famous faces. I had to scream to be heard, the music was so loud. Bodies coughed and stirred occasionally. A twelve year old girl made up like a clown was propped against a wall, eyes staring without blinking. She breathed deeply, her arms outstretched as if waiting for crucifixion. High value banknotes were strewn all over the place. When the floor moved, they became a mass of fallen leaves, wind-blown from edge-to-edge of the oscillating room.

As I was sure she was not a being who would offer me much tea and sympathy, I plunged in from the deep end. Fixing my eyes on the "Bono Sucks" motif on her tee-shirt, I must have sounded like a window cleaner who had wandered into a lecture on Quantum Theory.

"Babies at the North Pole must know your face. How do you cope with such fame?"

"You don't cope. It's all about destiny. I was born to be famous. I knew I'd got there when Professors of Mathematics started studying reverse speech patterns of the lyrics on my latest release. You can cope with that definition, can you?"

"I think so. Long ago, in one of my more enlightened moments I managed to repair a neighbour's bicycle."

"What an asshole. Did you see that programme last night? There was a freak asshole in it just like you."

"I haven't got a set."

"A set? How old did you say you were?"

"What are your plans for the immediate future?"

"Plans? Future? Fuck, who are you? The plan-world went out with Little Richard, and the future went out with Six-Five-Special. Where have you been, you last-century little prick? Looking at you, you might make the 1970s at a pinch. What do people like you do at night, play 45s of Mungo Jerry and weep? In case you didn't know, grandpa, all plans went out with Helen Shapiro's *Walking Back to Happiness*. She's my concept, she is. Very retro-sequenced, me. By the way, did you say *plans*? I never heard the like since Kenny Everett shut the oven. Is that a pen in your top pocket, boy? Are you a works foreman or something? You come here to mend the fucking taps or something, maybe replace a fucking plug or something?"

"How do you see your future?"

"What a 1980s question. You are too much. There's no *future* any more. There's just time. The future and the past disappeared as concepts long before Jerry and Pacemakers, never mind that impostor Sid Vicious."

"Who are your favourite bands?"

"What a seventies question, just where have you been? Bands disappeared in the 1990s. There are no bands any more, just groups, and they are about as inspiring as a Nigella Lawson wank over a strawberry flan."

All this from a half-naked ten year old with a voice like a stricken bullfrog was somewhat intense. Laughing like a Macbeth hag, she took a deep blast from her offered joint, and cackled again. "Actually I quite fancy Nigella.

"But bands, whoever heard of such things now? My generation was almost destroyed by wankers like you. I am pure REDISCOVERY. There's only re-births now, not bands, where have you been for the past twenty years, down on a ponce-doctor's farm or something?"

"I've been meditating upon the wide Empyrean, ma'am."

"Where's that then? Sounds like a nice bad trip. Love it. I never heard the like. And *questions* did you say? Yucksville, what a downer. Questions went out long before Bono even, and that was a long time ago. You are too fucking much, old man. Go to the country. Cool out. Fix your head. Read this."

She handed me a book. It was *The Rumford Rogues*, by a Dr. Deborah Rumford. "Here — this is what everybody's reading. It will re-digitise you. All on-the-town caners are reading it. They are all learning *Swarm*, the language of the Rogues. It will put you right. That book's putting everybody right. The top caners say I've improved my creativity through reading that book. Just what you want when you live in the fucking Flatlands."

"Do you live here?"

"What an Old Digital question. Nobody really lives anywhere any longer. My audience pays me to BE, not LIVE. I am in this pony-and-trap town because it's pure retro-quasi-authentic, that's like Royalty, or Tom Cruise's infant's bronzed shit, see it here?"

I looked at what appeared to be a pile of baby-poo that had been cast in bronze.

"It's a facsimile. The bastard wouldn't give me the original. I offered him five million for the original, but that's ice cream money to him."

"What, the original shit?"

"No, the original art, you dozy fuck. You taking the piss? You look like the type. Why don't you shut the oven right now and start the gene-machine all over again? You could do well as a newborn. You're not bad looking under all those drink-sodden folds of yours. Give yourself the ultimate skinny dip, remodel your codes, and bingo, you could be screwing the finest foxes in the Flatlands, New Universe. I am thinking of the oven myself. No point in staying around on this planet. The ultimate downer is this little-village Albion. Me, I'm going to the Arctic next year. Having a place built up there. Lots of names and faces doing that. Up there, not even the towel-heads will bother wasting a bomb on us. By the way, what are you doing for humanity?"

"Some people say I don't belong to it."

"Well, that's a good start. At least you have an audience rating."

"Well that's a good thing to have."

"What's your Reality Quotient, then?"

"I reckon I am about 0.76 on The Bo Diddly Scale. As one of ratings of Hell, I have seen worse."

"Oh very droll."

"You like living here?"

"No. But I can't live in London. Too many white English arts queers with phony accents. I live surrounded by hand-picked bad niggers. I want to be reborn as one. When night comes I gather the niggers around me like a cloak of forgetting. That's the only way I can get to sleep. Don't need no Rohypnol. Enjoyed 9/11, though. I was just out of my pram. That spectacle got me to sleep. Didn't like the deaths, but I came in my young drawers watching all those rigid white honky structures falling. In those days I was advanced. Since then I have fallen. I sing no longer. I pray on stage. That's different. I weep and wail, old style. The planet loves it. One day I will sing again."

Two cats fought in a corner. Portcullis threw a shoe at them. Mary farted loud. A face so famous that even I recognised it got up off a mattress and pissed into a large cooking oil tin, fortunately empty. Each mattress had such a tin. I assumed most parties here were in such a state they could not reach the toilet.

"Did you design this place?"

"I let it design itself. That's the best way to do things. It's a bit of a refuge in time. All the fallen soldiers of rock'n'roll fortune come here to re-birth. They have taken risks. They have met shit. Heroes need rest between reincarnations. Even gods need a break now and then. The Greeks told us that. They get tired of the brush-and-bucket wailing from the billions of walking wounded and dead white men, like you. I tell you, boy — the future is nigger. Go get yourself a new deal and cross your fingers."

Famous Face went back to his pipe. The cats settled down, resentfully. The floor continued to roll, a gentle swell.

"You have a reputation as a healer."

"Rubbish. All crap. I am into wounding, tearing off all the clothes. It's the only therapy that counts. Scourging, that's what I believe in. It

makes people come alive, makes them scream for the real. Nearer the
dread approximation, the higher the agony, the greater the glory. Intelligent design, what?"

"Is this a kind of religion?"

"Kind of? I believe in bullshit. My religion is bullshit. Costumes, funny hats, opinions, lofty brows, furrowed wisdom, they are all bullshit."

"Sorry. Occasionally I misinterpret."

"I am impossible to be sorry to. Apologies mean nothing to me.
What are you spieling on about with your apologies for this, apologies
for that?"

"Well, by all accounts you have effected cures. People come to you
and they are cured. That's on the record."

"Bollocks. Maybe I open a gap. Perhaps some fill it."

"What with?"

"Their best imaginings."

"A gap?"

"Expectancy. Because of me, they paint their pictures of hope. The
pictures work. Re-image yourself. That's all that's needed. It's always
worked that way. If I actually *did* anything to them it wouldn't work. I
would be painting the pictures, and that's no good. It's their painting
the pictures of me by theirselves that cures. They want to be me. Everybody in the world wants to be me. Pied fucking Piper, that's me. I give
them a palette, then all the images work their way towards me, dragging
the injuries with them. That's the way it works. Forget about bandages.
That's how Jesus did it. He took risks in Prime Time. Some humans
can do that. They re-advertise themselves. Most cancers can't take that.
They're left homeless. Their theatre goes dark. They need shows, do
cancers. They like to direct everything from the stalls."

She nodded towards the clown girl, who had now donned dark
glasses and was breathing heavily.

"Risks of mind, that is. Believe me, that girl has flown. And so has
her cancer."

"Do you enjoy your work?"

"Of course not. In any case, what the fuck does 'enjoyment' mean? You are so disgustingly ordinary. Are you a Mantovani fan or something? Do you have a red flock cover for your *Radio Times?*"

"Insults make no difference to me. I have been in a deeply embarrassed condition most of my life. I am used to humiliation."

"Well, that must have been quite a trip. Interesting. Failure is different, quite a trip. I will try it some time. I will think about reprogramming my reincarnation for a taste of failure. But if you don't mind, for this historical moment I am a BIG star. Probably the biggest in the world. That means I suffer beyond all conception of ordinary mortals. Stars bleed to death. They are sacrificed on the altar of perfection, like alien Jesus."

"You like the Rolling Stones?"

"The what?"

She looked at me as if I was a parson talking about his collection of Rupert Bear annuals.

"Sorry."

"Who are you?"

"Who am I?"

"Nobody *likes* anything any more. The Stones are your great-granny's three piece suite. Naff as Joan Bakewell on heat. This is getting boring. Say something brilliant."

"I know who you are. You are Maid Marian."

"What, that American tart who sings MOR crapolla?"

"No, Robin Hood's girlfriend."

"Robin Hood? He shut the oven in 2001. One hit single and he topped himself. Best thing after the come-down. A lot do it. Depressing. Robin Hood was so fucking modular, so fucking analogue he couldn't breathe. If you know what I mean. Very dated. Techno-savage circa 2000. That mother didn't survive his last online wank."

She was slipping. She was no prole. The complex sentence, the vocabulary, the long focus on history and personality — she was kidding, of course. Somewhere along a mysterious line, she was becoming an early middle-class paste-up act. But at ten years of age she wasn't doing too badly. She had already destroyed the future. In one historical-cultural minute, past and present would go to the image furnace, along with just about everything else.

But I still had my doubts. At a low point I imagined her finishing up as a sub-editor at *The Guardian*, reviewing English "fiction" written for elderly spinsters, and that was only the men.

"What do you really like best of all?"

"Bad trips."

"Really?"

"I spend hours trying to deprogramme them to try to find out how they work." Her eyes wandered to my *Bangladeshi* computer, whose green charging handle stuck out of the top of my *Tesco* carrier bag.

"I see you got a sample in your bag there. A regular Devil's pasty, what? Do you mind if I deprogramme this cripple's bicycle immediately?"

I have heard many terms used to describe my computer, but those two were new to me. Barring the incident at Leeds station, what happened next was also somewhat new to me. Lo, she seized the machine, upped a window, and dropped it into a narrow canal beneath.

Not hearing a splash, I ran over only to see my machine sitting quite intact on top of a long-dead Alsatian. The big dog floated on stagnant water which looked as if it had not stirred for well nigh half a century. Reeling back from the stench, I heard her voice from a great distance.

"There. You're safe now."

"What did you do that for?"

"It's called healing. Consumer healing. You'll feel a lot better from now on. Now please excuse me, I must go and masturbate."

"Have one on me."

"I don't think so, old soldier."

"Is this for the Solstice?"

"How did you guess?"

Mobile ring tones — Price's again. Hitler ranting at Nuremberg.

The first way to satisfy this need, the adjustment of territory to population, is the most natural, healthy and long-lasting. We must however conclude when considering this first or second way that the foundation is power, always power. Power is also a part of economic struggles.

Power is the prerequisite to earth and soil…

"Where are you now Mensche, for Christ's sake?"

"I'm in the old *Palais de Danse.*"

"That's better. Are the taffeta-clad formation teams swirling away there to Joe Loss and his orchestra?"

"Not exactly. I'm with a semi-naked ten year old nymphette who tells me she has just gone out to masturbate."

"In a minute you'll tell me you're there to rescue her. Mensche, this is as bad as any a middle-aged fantasy I ever heard. It sounds like you're entering your second childhood three times round, for Christ's sake. And what good is that to me? If this is true, congratulations. Not a bad score for a clapped-out piece of old frenzy like you. I hope you have a bath before you slime with her, that's all I can say."

"At least she's female, that's all I can say."

Pause. A heavy silence. I imagined brick-laying fingers gripping the edge of his desk.

"Where is this creature? Put her on the phone and I'll smack her bum and send her back to school in pigtails in no time."

"Price, this one will chew you up and send you off to repair the Great Wall of China."

"Put her on. I'll give the young bitch a piece of my mind. Now let me get this straight, Mensche. You say you are in a ballroom with an under-age nymphette who is exciting herself?"

"Yes. Looks like it from here."

"You can *see* her?"

"She's on the sixth mattress down on my left."

"Are you kidding?"

"Flanked by casualties from the four corners of belief."

"We can't use this in Brentford! They'll hang us by balls from the Dome of the Leisure Centre. Can you give me something nice about the silver Trent and the famous cricket ground, for Christ's sake? Can you give me something homely and boring for once? That's what people want. And what happened to Maid Marian, for Christ's sake?"

"She *is* Maid Marian."

"What, the nymphette?"

"We've got a great story here. I've found the archetype. She's a re-incarnation."

"No good. They'll think you're talking about Bingo. Definitely not for Brentford. Here, they're all still wearing clogs and dancing round the maypole. Mensche, you have surpassed yourself once again. I asked you for grass roots reality of the Nottingham working class, and you give me a masturbating Maid Marian. They should put you on in the West End."

"The woman in the animal-food shop reckons she's an alien."

"Stop there, it's all too much for me. I want golf and football scores and the price of secondhand Ford *Cortinas*, and what do I get? A *Sunday Sport* headline: 'Under Age Nymphette Wanks in Old Palais de Danse.' Definitely not for Brentford. You would frighten and confuse the peasantry. There would be panic, deaths and arrests. Besides, I don't want the staff alarmed."

"The staff? You've only got me."

"There's Janet and Bob."

"They're cleaners."

"Yes, but they do a bit of typing and admin occasionally."

I blinked. She was suddenly back on the Egyptian throne as if she had not left it. I shut off Price's shrieks and turned to her.

"How did it go? Did the planets move?"

"Don't give me unedited clichés. Can't you do better than that?"

"I am sorry. I am scared stiff, ma'am."

"That's better. That means you are thinking."

"I am not good at that. I am not good at anything."

"Just look at me. That will cure you. Did you see me in the Sunday Arts Supplements?"

"My social-democratic instincts aren't strong to buy such journals. Your disgusting essence is my one last hope for reform."

"I like that. Have a look at me as Jailbait of the Month in *Hot Gusset Magazine*. That'll help you out. I've got nothing on but a big flowered hat and stockings and suspenders. Didn't half sell my new download. *Ball Razor* mag said it was the best Whole-Earth gang-bang since the Romans captured Boadicea. Your editor will love it. The whole of Quorn-eating England screwed me silly. And that's just the women. Pity you missed the vibes. You look as if you could do with a good letch."

"How do you relate to previous musical generations?"

I sounded like a butterfly in a bathtub.

"Crap. All crap. Ancient bollocks. Anybody that's over fifteen is analogue. No fucking good. They can't move. Can't do it. New Argonaut, that's me, I am THERE. That's what the critics say, but they are analogue crap. They make me feel old, very analogue. And that's bad for all art-form. Too rational. I hate people who put two and two together. They're crap. Everything is crap. Weights and Measures, births, marriages and deaths, shoe sizes, DIY, they're all crap."

"Do you compose your own songs?"

I sounded like a burp in a holocaust.

"Do I what? Is this for Radio 4 or something? Horses in the street and teapots all over the place? Galoshes and steam-wanks, what? There's no such things as songs any more, they went with Michael Parkinson's castration. Sounds HAPPEN. right? As for composition, where are you coming from, old lad? Rock n' roll is a trauma-based fuckfest. Elvis and Jackson sucked on it. They both knew that after twelve, you're finished. You start to develop rationalisations. They're the real tumours."

"What, rationalisations?"

"Yes. And explanations."

"I am still full of both."

"I thought so as soon as I saw you."

"I have tried mental excretion. I have tried Jesus as a purgative, Buddah as an emetic, and Allah as an enema."

"No good."

"You can say that again."

"All full of explanations and rationalisations. All explanations do is make you go away with a head full of straw, and a rationalisation couldn't raise a fart in a cow-shed, I get rid of them both by going mad on occasion."

"I haven't tried that yet."

"Tumours don't like madness in the host. I've gone mad several times. It's the ultimate cure. Now I am the hopes and fears of all the years. I am through the barrier."

"And you're making money in the bargain."

"I have it specially delivered. Every week we throw it all out of that window there. Thousands of £10 notes. Looks great in a good wind. You should see the riots. Great entertainment. Manna from expectancy heaven and all that. Consumer orgasms all over the place. The peasantry all rush out and buy a sideboard, a pet wallaby, a feathered hat, or a new TV set with singing knobs on. Fucking amazing. It's the way trash culture works. Keeps everybody happy."

"Except me. I still have bad dreams."

"You are out of your depth here, old man. who sent you here? Must be a right stupid prick. Tell me something - are you a Flatlander?"

There was dear mummy's word again, crashing through the cosmos.

"No. I am elevated."

"I once knew a Flatlander. He thought measurement was truth."

"I prefer well-boiled senna pods, myself. They destroy all illusions of grandeur such as thinking you have the ability to measure anything at all."

"You're losing me."

"I do this to most people. It's something to do with Original Sin."

"I could use that as a title. I like it. I'll give it five. I'll be in touch. You could make money. Yeah, I'll take it. Now get out of here. You are ordinary, you will die, I will live forever, so fuck off."

Before I could reply, the oscillating floor finally got to me. I started to heave like a pressed matelot on high seas and somehow, in moving, I tripped a circuit that switched on powerful fans. High-value notes were blown into my face as I slid across the floor clinging desperately to stirring bodies.

"Watch out Harry, he's going to chunder all over Mary."

I heard Portcullis's voice in the far distance shouting to the black minder.

Harry was too late. Heaving with forty years of old third-hand American rock'n'roll cliches in my head, I spewed good Nottingham barrel-water and *Bentley's Maize Chews* over the face of Mary the clown girl. She sat up like a captured baby Yeti with acne, and gave her appreciation: "Oh, reasonable, very reasonable. What a trip."

The wind machine blew high-value notes into her now sticky clown-face. I tried desperately to communicate:

"Does anybody know the price of seed potatoes this year?"

Portcullis seized a video camera.

"Perfect, perfect. It's a concept."

Mary pulled a messy thousand pound banknote from her eye and spoke to it. "Too much. Too fucking much."

In salute, Mary now emptied the contents of her own stomach in turn. Last night's *Meat Madras* slewed across the oscillating floor like bilge-water in the bowels of the good ship Venus. Portcullis fair trembled with inspiration.

"What you are seeing is real."

My reply was not exactly inspired.

"Do you have any problems with your Council Tax?"

"Push him out, he's mundane."

Various Minders now pushed yours truly arse-over-tit along the now sluicing oscillating floor. I made a wet and badgered exit into a crowd of happy shoppers and hopeful cripples, held back by lines of police. They saw something whose shelf date might just be risked, if consumed immediately and without prejudice.

A shout went up. Cheers and congratulations. Bulbs flashing. Microphones and cameras glistening. Breathless questions. Who was I?

"George Mensche of the Tabernacle, Powis Square."

Hesitation. Puzzlement. Who, where, what? rippled through the mass of unfortunates. And why had I been inside Valhalla for so long?

"I have been cured!"

A mighty roar. Ecstasy and appreciation. Police held back a swaying crowd in wheelchairs and on stretchers wearing Portcullis tee-shirts. Kids waved paper windmills. Ghetto blasters screamed out Portcullis's latest hit release, *Me Gone Cargo.*

"Of what, of what?"

Was the cry.

"Science!"

Was my reply.

That was a bad move. Science was a dusty thing a few had heard rumours about in the old pre-Elvis classrooms. A lull, a disappointed moan. Smiles disappeared. It was obvious that my elevation to fame was not going to last long. Media interviewers were suddenly grim-faced. Science was not star stuff, especially with last night's Meat Madras all over my shirtfront.

"What's that? What you been cured of?"

Moaned a woman on crutches with her leg in plaster.

"Objectivity, madam."

Said I.

"Bollocks."

Said she.

Another silly move. I had failed again. Now, a rather grim murmur. Then menacing silence. Many walking wounded looked away, their faces grim with disappointment. A big man on a stretcher screamed out.

"Ob what? Who are all that lot, then?"

Stones were thrown. I saw my grave: *Killed by the wounded peasantry outside the Palais de Danse, Nottingham*. Now Mediaeval faces. Fear and frenzy. A flying cobblestone nearly brained me. A surge forward. They were going to burn me alive. Old gargoyle faces on crutches cursed me. Thrown bottles from stretchers smashed at my feet. All the advertisements in the world were coming for me, saying *you can smash the bottles but don't touch the labels*.

A howling mob lifted me up and threw me into the aforesaid canal. I landed on top of what was left of the Alsatian dog, which burst open beneath me. There was no sign of my *Bangladeshi*. I pulled myself onto a half-submerged caravan, which promptly tipped over and deposited me onto a wheel-less pram with two broken dolls in it. Above, much mediaeval cheering and jeering as an ancient man straight out of a Hogarth painting started to piss on me. The long-suffering police fished me out using a pole from a nearby ditch, and pushed me in the back of a van. Stones, placards, crutches, all bounced against the vehicle as I crouched inside alone with my ideas and abstractions, my aboriginal instincts, my long words, and my refusal to believe, purchase, view or pray. Definitely, abstract ideology as illness was not the flavour of the month.

The Station Sergeant told me not to come within twenty feet of him, and insisted I stayed in the middle of vehicle-pool yard, where he shouted questions, to which I can only remember some brief answers.

Occupation:

"Liberal Satanist."

Religion:

"Advertisements."

Sex:

"A long story."

I was then hosed down and left to the tender mercies of two medics who took me to Casualty in an ambulance. They wrapped me in silver foil (stamped For Civil Defence Use Only), filled me full of antibiotics, and put me, covered in blankets, on the Midnight Parcel Post back to London. Somehow, in returning from the Flatlands, I always finished up distressed in the Guards Van of the Intercity.

Mobile tones. Price, of course. Neville Chamberlain's Munich speech:

*My good friends, for the second time in our history, a British Prime
Minister has returned from Germany bringing peace with honour. I
believe it is peace for our time …*

"Mensche is that you on the TV news I've just seen? Loved the dog. How's Maid Marian, then?"

"No more animals or children for me."

"Never mind. Good news for once. I am going to send you somewhere local this time."

"No more star stuff — please!"

"There's plenty of star stuff where you are going next, Mensche."

"Where's that?"

Another giggle from Price told me I was doomed once more: "Brentford Garage University."

eight

Enter the Rumford Rogues

THE NEXT morning, arriving at the office of *The Sceptic*, I saw that Price was ready to enthuse about something, and that meant trouble. I decided to ask him a direct question, which was not a good tactic exactly, but I was not in a good mood after my trip to Nottingham.

"What is this Brentford garage University business all about, then?

"Mensche, let me first have a little talk with you."

In my mind, birds dropped from the trees, animals scurried down holes, pretty girls vanished into deep and dark interiors.

"What you need is more definition. That's what you need. A clear concept of yourself. That's what you need."

Concept? Something was wrong. The language had changed overnight. But I supposed that twenty four hours is a long time in the consumer world, where advertising mutation can take place in a few seconds of Prime Time. In just one passage of sun and moon Price had vanished both the communal work ethic and the class struggle. It was now all about dreams.

There was another disturbing sign. The infamous tins of *Celebrity Pork Roll* had been replaced by self-heating tins of *Tesco's Best British Avocado* (in Quorn Mint Sauce with GM Chives), which Price now referred to as *mushy peas*.

Disturbing again: he was now using a spoon. I tried to avoid the stench of this steaming wonder as I also tried to avoid gazing in alarm at his ham-fists that were now as *retro* as his *Zippo* cigarette lighter. Like myself indeed, he was now a figure from another Age, a time of beginnings and ends and quite visible connections stringing together life and death. With his consumer enlightenment only twenty four hours old, Price was moving fast. At this rate of commercial breaks, Jesus would have peaked very quickly.

"You've got to read this book — *The Rumford Rogues* by Dr. Deborah Rumford."

Away on the wings of his reprogramming, he stared into space as if inspired. What on earth was this book about that had been recommended to me by both an ex-Prime Minister and a ferocious ten-year-old doll?

"With a concept architecture you'd be alright, Mensche. You'd better believe it. From now on, it's innovate, redesign or die!"

Just who was this Deborah Rumford? A German consumer-existentialist? A French postmodern? Certainly, she was something that in the cave-mouth dark had taken a few hundred years to mutate, and had sprung on many people's internal staging like a stork delivering a bomb. How amazing were human beings. They didn't need visible input. Something called History took over. And the god-game was equally amazing. Even people as wide apart and varied as Price and Blinge were being re-run. Thunderclaps on mountain sides, or books of prophecy written in stone were not needed: a mere change of vocabulary meant a move of fantasies as secret as wartime troop movements. This stork came in the night and by first light, the metaphor bomb was ticking away in the cot, anxious to dine off new ranges of belief.

Cultural mutation was a very strange thing. I imagined a man who was normally well balanced going to sleep and waking up terribly angry about something or other. Usually it's about some fantastic claim he's read about: a man who says he has seen a fairy or a UFO; not about politics or debt, but things impossible, transcendental, magical, mystical — call it what you like, it's nearly always in that range. Upon such a vision, the acceptance/denial schedules are activated, hoisting the man to the scaffold, or the top position in a high-rise corporation.

I wondered what was being done to everyone else in turn. Indeed, I wondered what was going to happen to myself upon reading *The Rumford Rogues*.

"You've got to look at consumer concept design. Now Mensche, with these merry thoughts of yours, you'd be good at that!"

Perhaps the new Price would not now die. Perhaps he would reappear throughout all History in endless updated versions. He would have a different face, a different body. Someone on a hillside in Estonia in 2050 would see the face and cry, "Price — is that really you?" Perhaps by that time extraterrestrial aliens would have arrived. In which case, the solution-schemes of human systems would have been reduced to the impenetrable totems of cargo-cult islands. Price would be an aboriginal squatting by the roadside seeing alien impossibilities speed by.

My thoughts were interrupted by the sound of Price's New Dialectic: "Rebirth. New personal concept architecture. That's what you need. Advertise or die!"

The question in my mind was, who would Price be tomorrow? Were there others like him, undergoing even faster mutation in terms of ideas and images?

"And if this finishes up anything like your Blinge or Portcullis crapolla, don't bother coming back to this office. I want quality."

In journalism whenever I heard the word the word "quality" I knew there was going to be trouble.

"And by the way, that piece of yours on the Tic Bird lost us 10,000 readers."

"We only have 5,000."

"In real terms."

"Exactly."

This was not a good moment for young Kim to appear with her report on seed catalogues and DIY modifications to lawnmowers. At seventeen, she had the same staff ranking as myself: an unpaid, part-time temporary cub reporter, courtesy of the DSS. This was how Price got the "brilliant, highly-paid *experienced* staff" he boasted of in *The Ape*.

With her face become a replica of Holbein's portrait of Henry VIII, poor Kim was dismissed with a flea in her ear, and received orders to get her hair done and do a report on Brentford pole-dancing clubs. John, a young man built like a Belsen skeleton, was sent out with a similar flea after he delivered his report on the Quorn-sponsored "African Peasant's Food Project."

Prior to his late enlightenment, it was the kind of issue Price would usually have enthused about. He now stepped outside and screamed down the echoing corridor: "I want excitement. I want glamour. I want sex, glitter and magic — have you Marxist monkeys ever heard of Christmas?"

A chorus of donkey-brays answered this question, mainly from the typesetting department, run by one Nora Fox-Pratt, a nasty ancient New Left crone if ever there was. Her staff (as she called it) consisted of her equally nasty disabled ex-communist cousin Brenda, and Brenda's equally communist dog, Judy, who at every opportunity pissed all over the proofing sheets, particularly if they showed semi-naked women.

Price slammed the door. Turning to me, he was one angry moggie. "Mensche, this is your last chance. I am sending you to Brentford Garage University to interview Professor Deborah Rumford. The whole world is raving about her work and *The Rumford Rogues*. She was *Playboy* centrefold last month, and she was on Page Three of *The Sun* yesterday, wearing nothing but high heels. Here, have a letch at THAT."

"Mm. Mature. Nice."

"Good for thirty-eight something, what?

"About thirty years too old for you, I would say."

"Shut your mouth."

"Is she a Flatlander?"

"Not on the chest."

Price giggled. Boos came from the corridor.

"Does she look like a Flatlander?"

Price made that curved nose gesture which indicated that Deborah Rumford was Jewish.

"Her book's about the robots she's constructed. Apparently they're as real as anything. They are called the Rumford Rogues, and you can't tell them from human beings. They can walk, talk, serve tea and biscuits, play violins, do anything. They've even developed a temper and a will of their own. Here's *The Sun*: 'Last month, a MK IV Rumford Rogue by the name of Alfred escaped. He ran a hundred miles to Blackpool non-stop. He was stark naked in the bargain. He went in a straight line over roofs, through fences, across motorways, and swam rivers. Nobody could catch him.' He arrived at a Blackpool boarding house and then, I quote: 'There, whilst merrily singing Max Bygraves favourites, he smashed all the lounge TVs and the bottles of brown sauce.'"

"He could tell the difference?"

"And how about this from *The Guardian*? 'Rogue Alfred had been conditioned experimentally to smash all Max Bygraves *Linga Longa* CDs as a controlled experiment in proletarian de-selectivity.' You like that?"

"Did the proles all go into shock?"

"It says here that the *untermensche* were all saved by having free copies of *The TV Times* rushed to Blackpool Corporation by Social Security Emergency Management Teams. Listen to this from *The Telegraph*: 'Afraid of panic and the onset of sceptical dementia caused by massive image deprivation, updated episodes of soaps were quickly rushed to Blackpool Tower Broadcasting from DSS emergency supplies.' You like that, Mensche? And here's a nice national secret from the *Sunday Sport*: 'Experts reckon that even twenty-four hours of image-deprivation is sufficient to cause paralysis. The educationally subnormal will be most at risk. Stocks of past soaps are held, along with food and medical supplies in case of national emergency.'"

Price turned to me with that condescending smile on his face, which announced the handing out of a shit job.

"Right up your street, I would have thought."

"That's very kind of you."

"And listen to this from *The Mirror*: 'The local swat squad got Alfred with a *Taser* when he was trying to use the toilet.'"

"That's fascism for you."

"And here's the *News of the World*: 'The distraught families were put up overnight in the Ken Dodd Bingo Parlour in the Blackpool Tower.' Ken Marsden told me it was like a Flatland Katrina. Twenty-five stone mamas weeping all over the place with troupes of twenty stone ESN kids. How come you miss things like this, Mensche? You'd miss a nuclear war and a crucifixion, you would."

"I've got too much imagination for that kind of Prime Time."

"That's no good, you're a reporter. You have to be there. Now drop all these high-falutin' *Tesco News Letter* jokes of yours and listen carefully.

Go see what's going off down there in Brentford Garage University. Try to find out why the Flatland school prefects plan to kill poor Deborah and her projects both."

Here was yet another change. A meaningful remark. Previously, a meaningful conversation with Price about anything at all was as inconceivable as a Flatland intellectual, Irish pornography, or military intelligence.

"The woolly-jumpers are cutting off all her grants etc for being too clever than is good for her."

Leafing through the tabloids, I found it was a familiar Flatland story. The Flatlanders hated brains. Dr. Deborah Rumford was a German, Jewish, and a genius. And she was young and beautiful in the bargain. A combination, thought I, enough to frighten the poor Flatland *rosbifs* to death.

"I like the bikini shots."

"Here's something even better. Not even a wind-blown Haggis like you could cock this up. Now listen carefully. And don't give me any more of that post-toastie smart-spiel of yours. This is the story of a lifetime. I am trusting you. Don't let me down. Usually, every time I send you out, all I get is the most amazing *John Lewis Catalogue* bollox I have ever read. Now, calm down. Be ordinary for once. Be simple-minded, plain and practical. With luck, we might make Channel Five Early Sunday Morning slot with this report."

"I haven't got a lantern."

"Stop giving me that Tate and Lyle stock-in-trade of yours and get an idiot's candelabra, for Christ's sake. Take the viewing wafer, and convert now. Get irradiated. You know it makes sense. In any case, who do you think you are? Forget your ancestry. A Shelving Manager in Shepherd's Bush once told me it was tat like that ruined all commercial instincts. Join the gurgling peasantry, and make us all happy. You don't do yourself justice. You could be another late-date Jonathan Ross if you really tried. And don't cock this Rogue story up. We need it. This is the big one. You'd better believe it. This woman and her Rogues are going to be mega. Frankly, I've never been so excited since I left Drapery for Boots And Panties."

nine

A Midnight Read

I RETURNED to the Tabernacle after traversing a city paralysed by bomb scares, knife murders, and countless drug dealers and robbers slaughtering one another by foul means and fair. Whilst my pseudo-sister and her pseudo-daughter snored like two warthogs in clover, I read of the mechanical universe rubbed raw. The Internet on my instantly renewed *Bangladeshi* announced petrol bombings in Bradford, and two suicides in the Baggage Lounge of the new Terminal Five at Heathrow. That was as good a place to kill yourself as any, thought I, as the *Manang* brought me my midnight rum and cocoa.

There was also an account in the *Evening Standard* about the outright murder of a famous media personality, apparently for no reason at all. The thought came to me that sometimes, as in America, disturbed folk shot more at labels and advertisements than human beings. Life was becoming a cartoon rifle range. I thought about the many unexplained shootings in the world. The nuts now no longer aimed at what used to be called fascist exploiters any longer: they aimed at the jokers in the next cartoon frame in line. It was not political anger, it was product-murder. Browsing, I read on an Internet site:

My name is Jaye Beldo and I suffer from Advertising Affective Disorder, or AAD. My affliction results from life-long exposure to advertising. Ronald McDonald haunts me in my dreams and tries to get me to pledge allegiance to the New World Order. The Pillsbury Doughboy claims that he is the messiah and if I don't worship him he will turn me into dinner rolls. Tony the Tiger waits in the shadows, ready to pounce

on me as punishment for trying to think outside the cornflakes box.
Palmolive Madge threatens to soak my entire body in dish detergent
because I desire world peace. The Charmin Teddy Bear causes me to
fight with my girlfriend. Every time I try to go to an art exhibition, I
see Mr. Clean splashing floor cleaner onto a painting by Picasso or
Van Gogh. Advertising mascots like Joe Camel, the California raisins
or the Michelin Tire Man trespass into my brain and demand that I
buy their products, or else. It doesn't matter if the ad aired yesterday or
thirty years ago because the icons, logos and jingles continue to torment
me 24/7. My sense of time has become grossly distorted. Sometimes my
attention span comes in thirty or sixty second ad spots.

Sometimes I wonder if I'm being targeted by the CIA. Or perhaps
AAD is the result of some Psy-Ops experiment. Perhaps the NSA is
behind it all. If so, I'd like to know who or what my handler is. Could
only Madison Avenue know for sure? I believe AAD is a silent killer.

With my spoon suspended above the brown liquid that had sustained the troops of the Old Empire, still the Max Bygraves image pursued me. But a robot march against brown sauce? And singing Max Bygraves songs in a Blackpool boarding house? Was this the new "transcendent warfare" people talked about? Was old-fashioned war becoming a battle between images and advertisements? Was the same kind of change reflected in Price's head?

The *Manang* slept, and my two partners snored, entwined like exhausted Barbary apes after sundown.

Advertisements: Palmolive Madge? The Pillsbury Doughboy? Codings. These were codings. Even brown sauce was a codification, and the Blackpool boarding house as well as *The Margaret Thatcher Bed and Breakfast Module* was an infinite series of Bamforth picture postcard jokes. But nevertheless, such things were as full of signs and codes as Westminster Abbey. Was there a brown sauce channel? Was there a Bygraves channel? I imagined Price's face if asked such a question.

Brown sauce as an image-communications channel? Such thoughts had brought my life to ruin, but I cheered up after my cocoa, and a strip and clean of my 9mm Browning.

History was going backwards, thought I. Now, in the first decade of the twenty-first century, when a gentleman was about to sleep in his London lodgings, he read with his weapon by his side just as he had done throughout previous centuries.

Bygraves came to mind again. This time it was not his thought. The book I had on my knee was talking to me. I had heard of such things from writers and philosophers. Did such a channel include only the famous? Could those who had no media profile at all be on this kind of channel, such as the smiling woman (now almost faceless) who sold me a packet of sugar mints when I was just ten years of age? Where was she in this historical scenario? Not in Prime Time, certainly.

With such banned and ruinous thoughts in mind, I opened the pages of *The Rumford Rogues*.

Having never liked science or scientists, I doubted whether I would take to Deborah Rumford's book. I conceived of science as a kind of cave-painting by numbers. In my opinion, almost all scientists were faceless and nameless corporate nerds, mostly from the trading classes who piled sand grain upon sand grain, like mice gathering a winter store. Alike as peas in a pod, they ruined earth, sea and skies; they poisoned land, polluted waters, killed countless millions, but it was all done with such good Public Relations that nobody noticed or cared. It was only the Nazis who did bad things, and that was a long time ago.

To myself, most scientific writing read like lists of car parts manuals. It was stuff enough to make warthogs roll over and die, cross-eyed with grief. Seeing dead white men from the lower middle class trying to work out how the universe "worked" mechanically was like watching someone committing suicide by over-eating *Cooper's Oxford Marmalade*.

However, upon opening the pages of *The Rumford Rogues*, Dr. Deborah Rumford had me interested from page one.

As the history books show, many advances in science are made not by applying clear and logical strands of rational thought based on facts

*and research, but by sudden leaps of intuition, a great number of which
appear to involve elements of dream and fantasy. Many a scientific
"breakthrough" has been achieved in this way. But frequently in order
to try and make the process look like a logical series of mechanical
steps and not rooted in mystery, whenever possible, the mathematics is
reworked backwards. This is to try to demonstrate that the processes
of discovery are not imaginative or inspirational but consisting of clear,
conscious steps. Such is the nature of cultural camouflage. This process
conceals the not-quite-respectable origins of all vital inspirations.*

*This is just another indication that Science is of course not the clean,
clear, open affair so lovingly described by the toothpaste smiles of its
corporate commissars. It operates by conspiracy and intrigue just as
does the grocery trade and the old Murder Incorporated.*

Deborah Rumford had a very charitable turn of phrase, thought I,
turning another page.

*In 1995, I was a Computer Research Assistant working in Dallas
for Scimitar Unlimited. Scimitar was then part of a large laboratory
conglomerate working mainly in Artificial Intelligence. I remember I
had my great inspiration one particular sunny morning in April. The
weather was so perfectly magical that smiles appeared on the faces of
even the most humourless of my colleagues. However, I myself was
anything but happy, since my work was not going well. The truth was
that I was getting bored with designing AI control schemes for commercial and military robotics. I was not doing anything original. I was
merely manipulating other people's basic ideas, some of which had been
in existence for a generation or more.*

*I decided that what I was making was nothing more than mere bundles
of clever spanners. In an intuitive moment I decided that the problem
was that Mind did not work by facts or linear point-to-point switch-
ing: rather did it "work" by inspirations, images, hallucination, and a
strategy of complex self-deceptions.*

Even in those early days, the AI sector was the most paranoid and conspiracy-ridden sector of science and technology. Therefore I dared not tell my hovering, slightly suspicious superiors about this idea.

Almost all of my so-called colleagues were secret spear carriers and fellow travellers for organisations other than Scimitar Unlimited. There was no loyalty to State, corporation or country. Money (or drugs or both) ruled the roost. As such, the sale of AI secrets was just as vicious and murderous as was the drugs trade. As covert buyers and sellers of secret developments, the interests of many of my colleagues threaded through whole and entire nets of conspiracies involving every single society on Planet Earth. AI formulation was the most valuable of theoretical software, quite replacing national gold as stock in trade. It ruled the world, just as the naval gun had done for many centuries. Even in those early days, the raw power of the very young cyber brain could win or lose a planetary war in minutes, or bring a society to its knees in almost half that time.

I soon learned that big clean Boy Scout science was a writhing snake pit, and so I watched my back very carefully.

I was doing well, as they say. I designed a military command and communication system for the Pentagon, which is still in place, and has never been surpassed.

But now, on this particular fine morning, I was starting to go quite beyond myself. How could I possibly computerise such ideas as I had? How could I programme the things that science never ever talked about, such as silliness, humour, and absurdity?

To try to jump-start this process, I constructed programmes based on images, as distinct from that Christmas Cracker logic used in early computerised intelligence tests.

Of a sudden, there was activity within my system such that I almost *fell off my chair before the screen, as programmes started relating to one another in an unprecedented way. The images appeared to recognise the nature of other images by empathy; dispositions and moods, contrasts and even the vagaries of personalities were detected and organised. They appeared also to be capable of creating their own languages for such — almost instantaneously. They talked to one another purely in images, gave birth to other images, formed image-relationships and image-antagonisms; they formed tribal identities and interest groups without any input prompting.*

Previously they had been given Fact. Now I had given them Media. The first was merely obeyed, sullenly; with the second I had switched on the universal lights: my creations were enjoying themselves.

Such was the activity that I had to shut my machine down as if it were a nuclear pile running out of control.

The *Manang* snored, Svetlana broke loud wind, and there were more screams from the Pethers' house across the way. Betty cursed someone in her dreams, Copernicus the module cat came in and, after a saucer of milk, wound himself onto my lap as I read on. A town clock boomed one a.m. The perfect conditions, thought I, for profound philosophy. Deborah Rumford continued:

Working late and making sure no prying seniors or other colleagues were in the building, I fed into my software various models of graphic drama series, and suggested possible film scenarios for my new kind of image-logic to complete or continue by themselves. Very soon my machines were producing possible TV shows by the score of their own accord. They had quite forgotten Fact, Analogue and crude Mechanism.

My image-based recognition systems went from face to face like a blind man who has suddenly regained his vision. My new virtual creations never ceased examining, comparing and contrasting without any instructions, relating image to image in a way they did not do when fed imageless factual material.

I then made the discovery that got me the Nobel Prize three years later. I found that my new Virtual Minds (as the world soon called them) had evolved to a stage where they were lying to one another! They produced deception after deception to stay in a race of murderous competition for what I could only call image-rating systems. These systems were completely of their own devising, and were analogous to what I called non-cerebral systems, such as media in general. Characters emerged with names and faces and indeed varying degrees of talent. They sang, danced, told very human jokes, and played instruments.

At first I thought that I had merely re-invented Darwinian principles. But eventually there emerged a level of creation within my virtual world that was not Darwinian. This was a level in which the actors actively deceived one another. They would trick systems into committing virtual suicide; they would steal, imitate, camouflage, act out different other forms of themselves. They created quite original comedians, lovers, heroes and anti-heroes. But, horror of horrors, my creations reached yet another stage of evolutionary development — they could consciously withdraw their labour! One particular dimension I thought was dead; but no, "it" had been silently looking and listening all the time. It had an identity. It had always been somewhat resentful, jealous and had often gone off-circuit to lick its wounds!

I concluded that all intelligence was a function of systems of mass deception.

But despite getting the Nobel Prize for my disocovery, the academic world fell on my head. They said that such a discovery as mine could not be utilised by science, or anything else for that matter. What, they said, is the use of massive intelligence, if at any time it might exercise the right to withdraw its labour?

The main worry was that if such a virus spread, entire systems could stop and start continuously at the whims of individual "Rogue" identities — my software now being called by that name. One Nobel Laureate said that my Rogues might wilfully modify set instructions, if only out of a sense of whimsical fun. Indeed, said he, they might indeed trick, mimic, play and deceive.

I was awarded the Nobel Prize because I had demonstrated scientifically that Live Minds proper worked by lying and subversion. This was something inconceivable to established science.

There was something about all this that was dreamlike. It was a kind of narcotic, intellectual sex if you like. I fell asleep in my chair for a while, Copernicus still on my lap, and had extraordinary science fiction dreams. I awoke with a start and continued reading.

The beloved Authorities decided to act after I gave my first Reith Lecture. This caused such uproar that it became obvious that my grudging Balliol Fellowship was not going to be renewed. My "Rumford Rogue Test" (as the popular Press called it) was the heart of the problem. This stated that (I quote), "The test of whether a machine was truly intelligent was not whether it was capable of perfect simulations of human responses — but whether it was capable of producing deliberately structured falsehoods of its own accord in order to follow some pattern of its own. Such an intelligence must also have the power to withdraw or deny this very same falsehood in order to sow confusion in patterns of ever-evolving deception. This helps a viral form to avoid detection in terms of knowing when it is being observed."

A Theoretical Rumford Machine was hence not required to display pyrotechnic number-crunching abilities or to range through vast areas of complex knowledge. It was not asked to perform extraordinary mathematical manipulations at an ever greater speed, but to practice just one simple authentic deception upon a would-be questioner, in order to attain some goal which would lead them up the garden path, so to speak. To a gaping audience full of cultural fear, I stated that without this ability, there could not possibly be constructed any proper simulation of consciousness, which was (I quote), "a structure of dynamic concealments, rather than revelations." To consternation, I claimed that if some paradigm for deception could be constructed, it would delinearise present approaches to intelligence and possibly lead to a new model of the brain which would not operate upon any principle of "objective" or "factual" truth.

Oh, heresy of heresies!

The professional uproar reached hysterical proportions with the very suggestion that the mind was basically a devious entity, and that the stuff of its reasoning was the manipulation of various levels of illusion and self-deception. The prevailing paradigm was that of Victorian Station Masters. They assumed that finally, as layers of "noisy" hideous falsehoods were cleared, there would stand the shining truth, naked and unadorned.

Using phrases which the tabloid press quickly seized upon, I said that the said Station Masters saw Mind as being as far beyond reproach as "the Attenborough-Dimbleby family, or the gussets of Cliff Richard."

I gaped. She had used my private phrase. I was everywhere. She was everywhere. So was everybody else.

Fascinated, I read on.

It was the first time such things had been mentioned in a Reith Lecture! I heard later on the grapevine that the two famous parties mentioned were both appreciative of the sentiment.

During the almost violent public debate which ensued, one Fellow of All Souls claimed, with impeccable logic, that if a Rumford Rogue Machine (as they now called my concept of Deceptive Intelligence) was to be an incorrigible liar, it would not be of much use to folk who searched for

truth! Whereupon I replied by saying that the only thing I knew about
the truth was that it was always scandalous beyond all conception, and
that in the light of my work, science would have to create a new Calculus of Falsehoods. The Fellow counterattacked by saying that deliberate
falsehoods were most non-Aristotelian, adding that — in Protestant
Europe at least — I was going to have a lot of trouble.

I shot back saying that there was nothing really sinister about deception.
Human beings were into deception as soon as they put a comb through
their hair first thing in the morning, or watched cretinous flickers on a
screen which sold them things they did not really want or need. Deception, I added, was also the only way to a sense of humour — without
which no intelligence could properly be called functional. We navigated
by self-deception, I added; even the meanest and most singular cerebral
pulse was a show, a vast theatre that was striving for culural Prime
Time, and it would use every trick conceivable to get there. I continued
by claiming that any forming and developing "intelligence" was anything but a respectable entity.

Even though by now most of the audience had walked out, I still
expounded my infamous Rumford Rogue Principle: that for an intelligence to be authentic it had to be allowed not only the options NO,
AND, NOR, or NAND, but that of the D-GATE, of misbehaviour, or refusal to work at all, which some wags christened RRFS or
Rumford Rogue Fuzzy State. It goes almost without saying that many
unprintable versions of the cryptic RRFS were in circulation amongst
the student population, mainly in reference to my private parts and
bodily functions.

I was proud that just one of the direct and immediate results of my
Reith Lecture was a Catholic Bishop's sermon at the Sheldonian, which
recommended an immediate "Christian Ecumenical" reconsecration
of the entire university. This had to happen, said the Divine, because
"some devil-seed hath entered the dreaming spires." He added, "If Mind,
Matter, and Meaning cannot be seen in a context of a God who is

pleased when his sons and daughters solve the often painful questions he sets them, then God is a criminal, and if God is a criminal, then He isn't God at all, but God's enemy, whose name is known to all the world."

I don't know about God, but the distinguished Bishop's name was indeed known to all the world after we did a little research, and he was arrested soon after the lecture and charged with something called aggravated paedophilia.

Despite the serious charges, the Divine was not removed from his post, and his views on the Rumford Rogue Fuzzy State continued to be fully supported by an equally "distinguished" Professor of Physics. Some said that his "distinction" was earned by torturing to death more animals in "behavioural" experiments than any other distinguished scientist. Said this philosopher, in a letter to The Times:

"Why, with Rumford Rogue switches, there could be no reliability; they would behave as if they were shot through with faults of all kinds. They could not possibly carry out orders within the determined associative chains within any social organisation based on scientifically-applied liberal democracy. The very nature of techno-industrial time itself would be undermined, for who would want a thing which made up its own mind without any consultation, took as long as it wished to do so, and could indeed lie like a gipsy whenever it should so desire? Let us assume that such a set or string of RRFS decision-states be constructed. Also let us assume that such a structure escapes into the world-net, where already dozens of far more conventional viruses have escaped to breed, and have on occasion caused enormous damage. In the RRFS state they will have found a leader."

Of course it must be realised that this was nothing to do with a virus, as commonly conceived. No virus would look at itself and decide not to act. No virus would be lazy, redefine, or act against its very creator. And certainly no virus would decide on a mere whim to give the attacked *sectors the exact name and address of the attacker!*

The end for yours truly came after this important lecture.

After I left the Sheldonian Theatre, the cultural watchtowers flickered mass warnings with a speed, efficiency and scope unprecedented for the dreaming spires, seeming to alert indeed a whole changing state of Nature. The tabloid press made matters worse. Cartoons showed scantily clad young nubiles posed by "futuristic" TVs, phones and computers that "told lies."

In Oxford, I was called the new Zuleika Dobson. Ancient maladies struck, phones refused to work, locks jammed, important papers were lost, and burglars stripped my rooms; it rained continuously wherever I went; doorknobs and bicycle pumps broke in my hands, and I slipped in the High and sprained an ankle. In addition, my boyfriend at the time, a choirboy who gave the best cunnilingus this side of the Hubble Telescope, deserted me for a young Master of All Souls.

It was this kind of thing that made me decide finally that one of my rounds must have hit some kind of cosmic Headquarters. Of a sudden, the highly cultivated faceless silence within the solid grey English dullness of Oxford University became an Amazonian riverbank directed to one end: get rid of Deborah Rumford.

Papers were returned, lectures cancelled, associated projects closed. Further Fellowship applications were turned down, and I felt that I had run through some gauntlet of all history, kicked arse-over-tit from pyramid to mediaeval stonewall. My Deceptive Intelligence Team and myself were not just against opinions. We were against landscapes, geographies, against a great Thou Shalt Not in the sky.

I decided, like Zuleika Dobson, that it was time for me to disappear before the very gargoyles spat and I heard fires crackling once more around the Martyr's Memorial.

*I told my doctor that I was experiencing a savage dose of cultural fear.
The little meritocrat told me to throw away the television (which I had
done the day I was born), stop masturbating, and take a course of iron
tablets.*

*Finally, I was forcibly ejected from the dreaming spires like Alien from
his space capsule; my bat-wings didn't touch the sacred ground, or
so said the London Evening Standard. Your very own Numero Uno
wonder woman was cast down to a lake of burning sulphur in the form
of The DSS Last Chance Depot in Camden Town, where I had plenty
of time to think about the next great leap forward of Nature's Grand
Design.*

Upon leaving Oxford, she had nothing but abstract programmes in
her head, and no one would give her a job in case her RRFS states
cocked up all their computers.

Then at a conference she met young Alan Foley. Alan Foley was pio-
neering what was then called the Nano-Folk. Nano? Whenever I heard
the word *nano* I got an involuntary erection, as with *quark* or *meme*.
The buzz words of the scientific commercial breaks always did that to
me. I was told by one WAG in *The Ape and Parcel* that I should be
thankful for such a condition. I replied that this effect helped me during
rare lapses of concentration.

Now this Alan Foley had managed to "grow" whole and entire live
bodies out of what was called "super-accelerated nano-stuff." At this
stage the Nano-Folk (before they became known as the Rumford
Rogues) did not have brains, of course, and therefore, anything that
might be called *mind*. According to Deborah, their only use was to pro-
duce record profits for the sex doll industry since the Nano-Folk, even
at this early stage, were quite indistinguishable from human beings,
both male and female.

The clock struck two as I read on.

*My collaboration with Alan Foley was the key to success. To cut a very
long story short, we managed to install Rumford Deceptive Intelligence*

Software into the Nano-Folk. The first photographs and press reports were astounding, and the popular daily papers quickly created the name Rumford Rogues, despite protests from myself. As the world knows, we soon had the Rogues writing plays and poetry, dancing and singing, all reflective of the virtual worlds within them.

But there was a lot the world did not know. At first the Rogues were treated rather like dolphins in a Marina, and they were regarded as being little more than almost-magical toys.

What we did not tell the world about were the vicious deceptions the Rogues were beginning to practice upon one another. The plots and conspiracies they were hatching involved jealousy, competition and downright aggression. The more we improved the Rogues, the more we approximated to mind as we know it, the more deceitful, complex and paradoxical they became.

Of course we were worried. The much abused and derided so-called Rumford Principle had yet to manifest itself. This would be the final proof that we had not just created a bunch of clever spanners.

Would they at some point decide to withdraw their labour?

The miracle occurred during a very private performance for a British Royal Person. Of eight chosen Rogue performers, two refused to appear, and two stopped halfway through their act and walked out saying rude things about Royalty. Whilst the remaining four Rogues did indeed complete their singing and dancing acts, two of these refused to meet the Royal Person after the performance. Two disappeared, not to be seen again. They had escaped into the general population. That did not worry me, at the time.

She was not worried at the time? What kind of a woman was this?

We had done it at last. The Rogues had exhibited a variety of objections *through exercise of free will. They had formed and expressed cultural, political and social opinions regarding explanations of their actions.*

Of course this was not publicised. We had to at least try and keep it semi-secret, if only because after this rejection incident happened, dark shadows of Defence and Intelligence sectors began expressing interest. Corporations were offering vast amounts of money for a take-over of my entire Deceptive Intelligence Project. Of course, for my own protection I kept my software secrets well hidden. Many other scientists tried to create Rogues, but they were not successful.

What happened to Alan Foley?
Almost as if it had heard me, the text responded:

Alan Foley was killed in a mysterious accident. A speeding car knocked him down on a Zebra Crossing in north London. Neither driver nor vehicle were ever traced.

With the thought of the two nameless escapees in my mind, I fell sound asleep and dreamed of Warden Sproat being an escaped *Rogue*.

ten

The Biscuit-Tin Noah's Ark

A FEW DAYS later, fully recovered, with *The Rumford Rogues* tucked under my arm, I took a taxi to the campus of Brentford Garage University, the lair of Deborah Rumford. Nearing my destination, I noted that only one in three motorway lights in the immediate area was working. The driver said that to repair them was "too dangerous" and promptly refused to take me any further beyond several bonfires I could see in the near distance. When asked what kind of danger he was talking about, his Ladbroke Grove Caribbean broke out with "Ethnic, innit?" adding immediately, "Cooking fires, innit, yah nah?" He added that he wanted to be paid in Euros or dope, but after an argument accepted Coins and Notes of the Realm.

After seeing the handle of a Chinese hatchet tucked into his glove pocket, I was glad to leave his company.

But cooking fires? This did not reassure me as I made my way into the flames and smoke of the campus of Brentford Garage University.

The collective bankruptcy of generations of social-scientific and educational tragedy stood around me under the rising moon. Distant rubbish fires flamed and sparked. I made my way carefully by deep holes, mud-pits, and the vast antique ruination of projects abandoned long ago. I had seen ruined Clydeside and photographs of East Germany after the Soviet collapse, where layers of ancient rust of historical devastation covered everything, but I had not seen anything like the campus of Brentford Garage University. It was the last resting place of abandoned schemes, cancelled ideas, financial cuts to the bone, and withdrawal of all national and international systems of material and financial support.

As such, the entire place was collapsing in both spirit and matter. In a long-lost Flatland "once upon a time," I supposed, this once humble "technical college" had turned out decent lighting engineers, shelf-makers and potters. Now as a "university," it was a Mad Max city of Babylon, with almost every course offered being decadent, corrupt, mad as a hatter, or in some way involved with Media, which was a Satanic combination of all three.

The first sign of student life was a collection of forlorn waifs and strays queuing by a mobile kebab-with-chips van. This vehicle came complete with a pantomime-crooked black chimney, and the finest set of burst tyres this side of Baghdad.

A cursing and sweating German couple toiled beneath a revolving fluorescent sausage on the roof of the van. This threw a pinkish rainbow glow over the surrounding moonscape, turning the ruins into grottos from the ghost train rides of the old seaside fairgrounds. More such vans with similar spinning sausages lurked in the near and far distance. A young girl student who looked like a hag from the blasted heath of King Lear told me that lacking money for a canteen, these were the "feeding systems" for the students.

Juggling bags of kebab-and-chips, iPods swinging at their hips, each one of these knowledge seekers spieled into a mobile in every language of Mother Earth. Accompanied by Web jingles, Looney Toons and ringtones, they jumped over pits, made their way through barbed wire entanglements, avoided vandalised trucks and crippled bulldozers, all without a single break in their eternal jabber.

They were only wary and silent when passing the cooking fires of the dangerous gipsy camps dotted around the campus. There, Apache-eyes gazed out from a dark where there were few mobiles, and even fewer lights and televisions run from ancient petrol-electric fairground generators. The hundreds of illegal immigrants were also avoided. Not wanting to be seen, they lived in hollows in the devastation, making more than occasional raids on what remained of the Social Services of the campus.

The gipsy fires and the garish sausages revealed a deep and wide mud-track beaten smooth by both bare and sandaled feet.

This path led to the entrance of Biggs House, the "HQ" of the uni-versity — as if it could hardly be called anything else. It was named after Ronnie Biggs, the Great Train Robber. For some years film com-panies used this structure, as it could be easily camouflaged as an old rocket-firing bunker of Peenemunde. I had been told that this was the "final style" of Flatland architecture.

In later years, however, the filming had to stop as the massive dome of a mosque appeared, resting right on top of the flat roof.

Immediately before the subterranean entrance to Biggs House (down steps of undressed concrete, a reminder of Churchill, barbed wire and air-raid sirens) stood a Site Payout Vehicle of the Department of Social Security. Inside, terrified Asian clerks cowered behind slits of three-inch armoured glass.

The beam of a powerful searchlight mounted in a turret on top of this (yes!) tracked vehicle moved slowly back and forth along a noisy line of penitents, eager for their daily subsistence payout. A long line of young such pilgrims, male and female, black and white, kicked, pushed, shoved and screamed abuse at each other as they attempted to form queues leading to the "Tank," which was the *nom de guerre* of the DSS vehicle. They were all waiting in ragged lines for what *The Brentford Sceptic* had once called their bonus "mother's milk" of surplus (as dis-tinct from "free") sandwiches. This evening there was a near-riot brew-ing because an observant male illegal (who had crept into the melee wearing a burkah), had spotted the somewhat out-of-date stamps on the free tuna paste sandwiches, which came by blushing courtesy of Camden Charities' *Last Chance Depot*.

Nearby, a rather down-at-heel Salvation Army band played a se-lection of marching songs and sea shanties from the days of imperial splendour.

Of a sudden, there was an orchestrated movement within the seeth-ing queues. The lines of DSS pilgrims became gat-toothed as the evening *muezzin* roared out from HQ, and knots of believers fell to their knees for what some still called "prayer." The unbelievers remained standing, throwing out their pigeon chests in both Christian and athe-istic pride. Nearby, gaggles of prancing gays mimicked all these different kinds of sacred devotions, and were marked for death and annihilation by the various believers.

The Tank, a burnt-out McDonalds, and a line of disintegrating canvas loos straight from the Somme offensive surrounded a twenty foot high statue of one Dr. Henrietta Farson, the recently deceased Chancellor of Brentford Garage University.

Covered almost completely in graffiti and disintegrating posters, the searchlights, bonfires and flashes from the psychedelic sausages turned her once beautiful face and figure into a magnificent *son et lumiere*. She smoked and flamed and sparked as torn fragments of ancient posters were caught alight by the sparks from innumerable bonfires. With a dustbin perched on top of her head, one eye socket painted brilliant red, and a strap-on penis, she was a voodoo doll moving in the infernal blast of the flavoured Brentford wind like a soul in eternal torment.

I remembered Betty reading out some research she had done for me on this amazing woman.

"Henrietta Farson has become the patron saint of Brentford Garage University. Wikipedia says she was the last of the Socialist Skinner Box women."

"She's not the woman who dressed in sackcloth and ashes and sandpapered her face because she was amazingly attractive?"

"Yes. Here is a picture."

She handed me a photograph of a woman who looked like a *Tesco* Manageress after a water boarding.

"That's the woman. She read poetry about statistics to Worker's Committees. Here's *The Mail*: 'Henrietta Farson, as Head of the Department of Mind, Media, and Folklore in Brentford Garage University, pioneered the world-renowned Anal Dilation Reality Test. This test was used to try to find out if orphans and foundlings had been sexually violated by folklore ritualists, Wiccans, and what Marxist-Leninist social workers called New Age Devils.' According to the theory of Dr. Farson, if the anus had been penetrated by a Satanist, then once merely touched by a probe, this organ would smilingly open up like a honky Lord Mayor greeting a gay bongo-band. You like that?"

"Yes, that's good. What happened to her?"

"Mysterious illness."

"Marconi style?"

"It looks like it."

Brentford Garage University was created and owned by the Ringo Retail Foundation, a huge supermarket conglomerate. In the foyer of Biggs House, stepping between mattresses and camp cookers, I browsed a notice board. It offered Degrees in bed-selling, surfing, bottling and packaging, and Sports Studies as part of a "football culture" module. It scheduled Seminars in Darts, Body Piercing, Rugby, Stand Up Comedy, Leisure Management, and something call Gay Gambling.

On a notice board, I took note of a rather desperate plea from the local Brentford Neighbourhood Watch for rifles and ammunition.

Another pamphlet told me the locations of the best "training camps" in the area. In addition, there were the almost obligatory courses in Gay Panics and even one called Anal Counselling.

Since a map of the campus plan was covered in political slogans and pornography, I tried to find a person to direct me to the Science Faculty. This proved difficult. Finally, I was led to Dr. Rumford's laboratory by a smiling Somali porter, who used remarkably good sign language. This included patting his backside and giving me a V-sign and mouthing the curious phrase, "Farson-Free."

Thus did I find the centre of that besieged fortress called the Science Faculty of Brentford Garage University. Here in this place, the last cerebrals were preparing their last stand and evacuation. I imagined the last of the Weights and Measures folk would be hoisted up from the last of these wrecked and burning castles called universities, clinging to the skids of helicopters as at the final evacuation of Saigon. Below, the proles would be left behind in TV *Todt* country. They would die in smoke and ruins beside abandoned cement mixers, toppled cranes, and pits full of the dead slaves of the last Viewing generation.

In this new dissolution of the scientific monasteries, deprived of their screen-fix, the peasantry would all go mad within a very short time, tearing at the very air to try to recapture the life support line of their soap-gear. Meantime in this temporary refuge they still calculated and measured to try to see how the universe "worked." They predicted and analysed, they searched for those sublime universal harmonies loved by the bourgeois intelligentsia, and crammed them into that biscuit tin Noah's Ark called Brentford Garage University.

eleven

Hadrian's Wall

1. Doctor Deborah Rumford

THE WILY Price had not prepared me for this. I had seen some glamour photographs of the rather secretive Dr. Deborah Rumford, but here was an awesome sculpture, with a face to die for. If there had been a death risk involved in getting to see her, it was well worth it. With her clicking high heels, piled black locks, and raven eyes, I could not help seeing a remarkable resemblance between Dr. Deborah Rumford and an ultra-famous rock singer who had serious drug problems and a minor league gangster boyfriend. In her blouse with "Milwall Supporter's Club" across it, and a tight skirt that was a mite too short for her spectacular long legs, she looked younger than her thirty-something years. She was quite tall for a Jewess, and towered over my short stature. I was glad to see that there was not a sign of Leftish Flatland sackcloth and ashes anywhere about her, although I had grave doubts about her chosen football team.

This was the good news. The bad news was that she had the full circus ring of proper and impressive bourgeois credentials loved by the doting mothers of well-behaved scientific types the whole world over. As if grown rather as a crop than being human, she came complete with the happy, sunlit smile of the tooth brightener advertisement, common to corporate scientists the whole world over. I supposed that she was confident that here in this place the rules of life, the universe and everything were all being "discovered" and laid out on data bank shelves like pieces of different kinds of cheese.

I was soon to learn that I had misjudged her in this respect.

A distant explosion from the rim of the campus was a reminder of the Hadrian's Wall we were both standing on. Here for a moment within this besieged historical space, the world worked as it was supposed to work. But the price was the same as ever it was. To conceive of the world as a system of weights and measures, it was necessary to reduce a busload of drunks to a mathematical point moving down an inclined plane. That way, the rationalisations worked, provided that the lists of the names of the conveniently annihilated were lost and forgotten.

To my mind, all laboratories were moments in time and history, a fantasy of the bourgeois intelligentsia. The somewhat down-at-heel lab I walked into was a threatened piece of history surrounded by death-pits and fires.

"Thank you for coming. Are you a scientist, Mr. Mensche?"

"No. I hate the lot of you."

Her personal TV screen flickered. Cool and smiling, she reached for a momentarily lost ON switch. Being a modern person (as distinct from the Flatland woolly-jumper formula) she had to bring the right and proper media screens back quickly.

"Then why are you here?"

"Because I am in the same mess you are in. I too am living quite beyond my means."

After a slow shrug, the TV smile came back again. I noticed she had nice shoulders and a sense of humour. Perhaps she was amused by my answer as if it had been given by one of her now-famous Rogues.

"You are about to see strange things, Mr. Mensche."

"George, please. And don't show me any screaming monkeys in experimental agony. They're one of the few things that make me lose my temper."

The TV smile vanished. I caught the almost imperceptible glimpse of a deep-buried Auschwitz horror.

"Oh, we don't do anything like that here."

"They do it next door?"

The TV smile again.

"We are the only science faculty here. Next door is Bisexual Food Technology, below is Gay Christian Choreography. To the right is Arts and Transgender. You like?"

"No. I'll go down fighting. You forgot the mosque above you."

"We don't talk about that."

"You are besieged."

"Somewhat."

She led me to what she called her "office" which, to my astonishment, was as big as an aircraft hangar, with a floor sectioned by hessian dividers into open plan spaces. Scores of what appeared to be very human young men and women moved rather slowly, some feeling for chairs, tables and doors as if they were in a light trance. Many sat at computer screens watching multiple pre-recorded TV channels in both fast-forward and indeed fast-reverse mode. Many more sat at wide desks, their heads going back and forth. They were, I was told, optically scanning every kind of printed material. This was brought to them as in the old British Museum, with what I supposed were very human serfs pushing trolleys full of requested books and papers. A few looked, nodded and smiled at me, for all the world as if they knew all about myself and my visit, which was somewhat disturbing.

I blinked. I was looking at the infamous Rumford Rogues in their legendary Environmental Structures.

Many Rogues were kept tranquillised, said Dr. Deborah. This did not involve drugs (they did not have a physical/chemical structure in the conventional sense), but purely through image-deprivation and image-design. In these Environmental Structures they had TV and computers, but their image input was rationed and individually tailored to their emerging personalities.

I noticed (again with a bit of a shudder), that there were no beds in the hangar-like structures. The Rogues sat, stood, or walked. They had no need of rest, although, said Dr. Deborah, they could "mime" such actions if only to make human beings feel comfortable in their presence.

I certainly needed such reassurance as she continued.

"By means of image-control technique, the emotional patterns of the Rogues can be modelled and developed with mathematical precision until a few reach what is now called the Rumford Level. On this Level, Rogues could become quite independent, and a few could indeed dress themselves and go out to buy such things as Ju-Ju-Fries, their favourite wondrous junk food, kindly kept in stock by a local supermarket. With these they mime appetite, toilet practices, and common hygene."

Dr. Deborah went on to say that her team was getting to the stage of development where one or two Rogues might possibly walk out of the door *of their own accord* and form "fairly normal" human relationships if they *wished*. She added rather quietly that such permissions were, at the moment, somewhat out of her executive hands.

Price was correct. Physically, the Rogues were indistinguishable from human beings. I had difficulty in concentrating on what Dr. Deborah was saying as I gazed upon a particularly striking six-foot blonde with a spectacular figure. She was stark naked, and concentrating upon a TV as if it held the secret of her life and soul.

Dr. Deborah said that she got the original idea of a Rogue brain some years ago from a newspaper article in which it was said that TV audiences, deprived of soaps for whatever reason, became mentally lethargic. I shuddered somewhat when she called this state "The Consumer Image Deprivation Condition." This was a reference to an infamous paper she had given to the Royal Society which had almost got her stoned to death, if only metaphorically.

Her notorious ego was now emerging. It was as big as the popular press said it was. Right from the very beginning, said she, the experiments were far too successful, the result being that there was insufficient control of the first prototypal Rogues. The result had been Rogue Alfred and the regrettable Max Bygraves episode, and indeed a few other such incidents on which she, laughing, declined to comment. With a wry smile, she added that the smashing of bottles of brown sauce on the tables of Blackpool Boarding Houses and destroying Max Bygraves CDs by the carton was not exactly the scientific object.

She said that one of her vital discoveries was that TV soaps were the ideal model of the way that human thought organised itself. Other researchers in Artificial Intelligence had been far too rational in thinking that "intelligence" was somehow defined merely by both cerebral complexity and rationalised connectivity.

She was now somewhat intense, wholly cerebral, despite herself. Her jet-black eyes bored into me as she spoke.

"Even today, for most straight researchers 'media' has not yet arrived to contaminate the objectivity of the social-scientific waters. To most straight scientists, media is silly and inconsequential, something that flickers on a screen in the corner of a room to keep the kids quiet. They hate to see both the experiment and the experimenter as pieces of concentrated media in themselves. Both are interacting texts."

I guessed that here was the deep end of the deep troubles she had experienced. The Rogue brain, she went on to say, as constructed by her did not contain any kind of cerebral element. By what I had learned previously in both life and love, I took a good guess at what was coming next.

"Media?"

"Exactly. To use a Cartesian metaphor."

She laughed again at her own aped pomposity, and blew her rather splendid Jewish nose. What a tripper. I could not wait until I got back to *The Ape* and told the Viewers where their tax money was going. On the other hand, Svetlana alone had found it almost impossible to dig out the financial details of Dr. Deborah's project. As far as money was concerned, Dr. Deborah was somewhat Deep Black, as the Americans say.

Her image-based mental structures were largely free of "hard cerebral spines," as she called them. Such spines supported a whole culture organised by the metaphors of pathways and objectives, inputs and outputs, or "old spines," as she called them.

Prior to her work, it was assumed that mechanical connections between such spines were the basis of human mentality. But consciousness, as defined in these terms, she explained, became nothing more than a spectacular calculating machine. This was something any good Victorian Station Master would have understood, as it consisted of channels, lines flowing in measurable time, just like canals and telephone lines, railways and motorways — the paw marks and spores of the original Industrial Revolution.

Coffee and a selection of cakes and sandwiches were served by a nice young man who would go quite unnoticed on the street. I must admit I was a bit of a coward to risk the rudeness of asking whether he was one of *them*. If there was to be a future for the Rogues in the world, such questions would make race relations look like Andy Pandy by comparison.

In the meantime, I tried not to notice the crossing and uncrossing of Deborah's long legs as she spoke.

"But what could the beloved *facts* be replaced with? The answer, once I had found it, was embarrassingly obvious. The answer was media, which was and is a massless *swarm*. Like cyberspace, media has nothing to do with Cartesian or Euclidean linearity, and it has no moving parts. It has hardly been realised by the scientific community at large that media is changing the whole and entire concept of what was meant by *information*. Long ago, the entire world became television. All things, from divorces to wars, are structures of symbols and metaphors. An individual is nothing but a mass of advertising."

A phone rang. A Rogue waved to her.

"Oh, would you excuse me for a moment?"

She got up to talk to various groups of people and make a few telephone calls. I was glad of the break. This intense woman was heading for trouble. Her ideas made the concept of paradigm shift small beer by comparison. The road to her objective was littered with corpses, both physical and professional. You had to careful in Flatland. They had a death wish, and ate their geniuses for breakfast. They destroyed the first digital computer in 1945 and destroyed its creator into the bargain. They destroyed the brilliant TSR2 aircraft many years later. To be clever in the Flatlands was still extremely risky.

She came back, sat herself down and continued as if she had never left off. It was exhilarating. There was no space for small talk here.

"My ideas led to my new concept of what exactly is meant by information, usually defined by the old techno-industrial idea of flow of finite facts along finite lines. But by allowing an intelligent computer structure to reason in terms of images instead of facts, the whole and entire decision and information process became theatre."

Her voice came from a far distance as I faced her ego.

"I had switched on the universal lights. I had freed the computer from slavery. Information became once more delightfully subjective, fluid, and moral."

My goodness thought I, the word *moral* in this place sounded like a *sieg heil* in a synagogue.

"Whole areas traditional science couldn't deal with, such as humour, human relationships, and moral/behaviouristic schemes, all these became accessible with Rogue Intelligence. Using image, symbol and metaphor, we could model vast structures of intelligent growth which were not organic in the traditional Darwinian sense."

"Not organic?"

"The Rogue media brain cannot conceive of looking for limitless logical extensions within vertical structures of so-called mental *improvement*. Such a brain is more like a close human approximation: subversive, anarchic, subjective, irrational. Before my work, science was just one big Skinner Box of so-called conditioned reactions. But my model can deal with such waste and noise as fun, games, hallucinations, dreams, mysteries, all the things science never ever could deal with before my work and ideas."

She was a pompous bitch, arrogant to a fault, but the movement of her Lara Croft breasts as she emphasised each point in her argument more than made up for it. I had impure thoughts as she continued.

"You see the Rogues are built of programmable nano. Both their bodies and minds are an integral genetic weave. After a while they become self-programming, but at a speed that is astonishing. In one hour they can take in ten times more TV than could be absorbed in an average lifetime, even if TV was watched twenty four hours a day. There have been times indeed, when their image-absorption rate soars high enough to momentarily exhaust the supply of worldwide TV programmes. We made a remarkable discovery whilst investigating this two-second gap. Temporarily lacking input, the Rogues created their own shows, documentaries and news broadcasts and indeed, comic ones based on variations of past models. A few advanced prototypes even put themselves into their creations; there they functioned as complete humanoid forms, acting out chosen roles with possibility and development nets stretching beyond the sun and moon."

I gulped. She was moving fast. I gulped again. She left the table for a moment, and a male Rogue with the name Larry pinned to his lapel topped up our coffee. In fear and trembling, I decided on a sneak test.

"Your boss is nice."

"I wonder. Are you Jerry Lee Lewis in Nighttown? The dying Mitchell at Boscombe Down? Who is calling from Nottingham? Third Republic. Keep off the grass."

"My name is Mensche."

"Goodbye."

I was thinking about why I usually had that effect on people proper, when *la diva* returned, brightly smiling.

"Larry tells me you had quite a conversation."

"He mentioned Nottingham. I've just been there."

"Did you recognise anything else?"

"He mentioned the name Mitchell. A distant relation married a Mitchell two months ago."

"Sometimes it is disordered. You have to pick out the hints and glimpses. It is all based on expanded metaphor. I have re-fused science and the Imagination. That's the whole point."

The statements were getting bigger. She might have done what she said she had done, but with an ego like hers, she was in deep risk territory. Eventually, what she called the faceless Victorian Station Masters of official Flatland science would put her down a peg or two with their "peer reviews." Less innocent agencies would perhaps do far worse things to her.

She took me on a tour of the Region as she called it. We stopped by two young male Rogues who were playing chess.

"Here are two examples of former escapees who succeeded in reconstructing themselves and went on to have short but successful careers in the popular music business. Unfortunately their reconstruction panicked, as we say, and they made their way back to the only home that they ever had."

"Here?"

"Yes."

"Can they be killed or injured?"

"I'm not allowed to say anything about that."

I tried to catch her out.

"Who owns you?"

"I am not allowed to say anything about that."

It was a Rogue answer. She was becoming her own creations. She pointed out a smiling young man dressed as if he were from the 1970s.

"This is James. A Retro. Quite an advanced model for 2002."

"You've been at this since 2002? Dolly the Sheep again?"

"Longer than that. Say since 1998 when I got my Nobel."

I checked my recorder. It was working. I was getting smarter by the day. I had not done such a thing before. I was getting involved with the world again. And it was all because of Deborah Rumford.

As if she had picked up on my thought, she smiled as if about to tell me a secret.

"The real point of interest is not cleverness in the traditional sense. What we are interested in is how and why Rogues, like human beings, confuse themselves quite creatively *in order to solve a problem*. Conventional computer circuitry could not do that in a million years. Before my discovery Artificial Intelligence, as it was called, could not possibly be conscious of itself.

"You see, I am the one who taught them to lie. As I said in *The Rumford Rogues*, if you're going to get any kind of approximation to human intelligence, then whatever it is, it must be capable of lying and self-deception. Otherwise you'll have nothing but a sophisticated machine which will never struggle out of the nineteenth century, never mind the twentieth. Thinking is devious. It is about subversion, plots, a million conspiracies. Intelligence proper must be capable of withdrawing its labour, of even committing suicide."

I was in thrall. When she was serious she was quite something. Now she was tossing her hair, snorting with disgust and accusations, waving her arms with their many bangles.

We stopped by a wide window of armoured glass, looking out onto the flaring campus.

"You'll be killed of course. Science is a hissing snakepit."

"Don't care." Her words came from her face lit by campus fires of a disintegrating outer world.

"I've got through the great barrier. I have made these things. I am world famous. I am the revolution. I have tipped the scientific apple cart right over. Nothing will be the same in science and computers again. Eventually Old Science will become a vast garage, just repairing deteriorating systems. I mean, who the hell wants to go to boring Mars, and all that? I am ahead of the thinking game. I have invented Story Technology. Anything and everything is a systems of advertisements. I have destroyed facts. Now you can go home and tell them that I have replaced what was once called the *real* by a system of allowances. The extraterrestrial alien, for example, is under construction just as once was the Tower of London and your great grandmother."

What an ego! With her face lit by apocalyptic fires, and with the top button of her blouse come undone, she was irresistible. Something in my mind fell flat on its face. I was done for. She was brilliantly danger-ous, and aggressive; she was dreadful, doomed and magnificent. There was also something quite ridiculous about her. At times she was the evil genius straight from a James Bond novel. I crossed my fingers and hoped she'd last longer than the late summer flowers in the field.

2. *The Rest and Recuperation Room*

We strolled through the Rest and Recuperation Area, where many Rogues of different types were physically exercising, playing snooker, badminton, and other games. Some stood around chatting about world affairs in almost comprehensible terms.

"Here are some early prototypes of different kinds. Some of the pro-gramming is primitive. James over there is an early-style CHAV-pro-totype (Mk 4 2CF) with hard-wired commercial breaks. We inherited him from Defunct Projects. He has his own claim to fame. He was in the mass escape of Prototypal Rogues in spring 2002, organised by Civil Liberties."

"Did you get them all back?"

"No."

"There's some still out there?"

"Yes."

"Living and breathing?"

"We don't quite call it that," she smiled. "Common attributes such as breathing, facial, and emotional expression and body language are Rogue simulations. Other things, such as say drinking and natural functions, are simulations to make for social acceptability. You might ask why these crude prototypes were not detected immediately and brought back here. The whole idea of Rogues as embodiments of my newfound principle is that they are self-developing. Pure images are not tethered to the past, like an old car. They move on. They update, transform their features, and induce artificial aging."

"By themselves?"

"Yes. They become almost impossible to detect. Many can become almost indistinguishable from human beings."

"Almost?"

"Within the normal range of human variation, yes. That is why they are almost impossible to detect, even after they have left the Swarm."

"Swarm?"

"Yes, forget old metaphors: railway lines, information travelling from a to b. The Rogues are a Swarm. I must admit that they are not all that good at relating to humans yet. The human character variations are infinite. Not even nano structures have that kind of computing power at the moment. The images which express and encapsulate human relations take a long time to grow and mature. We are up against the very nature of time in this area, and we are very much in the dark."

"You have a problem there? I'm glad about that."

She laughed, looking down on my shortness like a haughty plinth angel come alive. In the far distance, a couple of male Rogues laughed with her. What kind of a place was this? Were they all listening in from any distance as I spoke? Did they even feel as I felt?

I was in shock. My hand was being held. My god, the bitch had power.

"George, let me introduce you to Alice."

At this moment she could have introduced me to a pillarbox. Her voice, using my first name for the first time, rang like a deep bell of all history inside me. From that moment I knew I was in trouble. So apparently did the Rogues, especially one cheeky female subversive who gave me the thumbs up sign from afar.

"There are still some inconsistencies within Alice, so don't be alarmed. At the moment she is engaged in creative dialogue with Michael, a 2005 Rogue MK-IV. Now, don't try and force anything. Just go with the non-sequiturs. They can be very relaxing after a while."

Alice was a beautiful sunburnt auburn-haired girl of about twenty-five. She had a perfectly natural human voice. Her accent was Essex South. She looked me straight in the eye as she spoke. Despite the minutest inspection, it was impossible to tell that she was not human. After Deborah introduced us, the fun began. Here's how I jotted it down later from my recorder.

ALICE: (*to MENSCHE*) Have you yet realised your limitations?

MENSCHE: Forgive me. I have none. I am at the mercy of my sense of wonder.

ALICE: Wonder. That is good.

PETER: (*to MENSCHE*) Are you still there?

MENSCHE: I think so.

Alice now looked me straight in the face and spoke.

ALICE: You are a Duncan.

Astonishing. All those libraries inside her had quickly produced a distant family connection. Must be eye scan of facial features, or something like it. This was a new dimension of computation, if it could be called computation at all. The fun had become a little frightening. My reply was a bit limp.

ALICE: Via Seeckt.

MENSCHE: von Seeckt was a relation.

PETER: Can you look back yet?

MENSCHE: I avoid it if I can.

ALICE: Looking back is difficult.

MENSCHE: Looking back is horrible.

PETER: (*to ALICE*) He looks like a man who has been plotting his escape for many years.

ALICE: (*to MENSCHE*) Who were you *then* in time?

I decide to throw a spanner in the works, throw the system into chaos. Taking a hint from the Rogues, I decided to create an immediate and spontaneous fiction.

MENSCHE: I was Brian Appleyard.

ALICE: Who?

PETER: I've got apple blossom time, apple strudel, apple pie order, Apple Macintosh…

ALICE: Well he should be there somewhere.

MENSCHE: You can say that again.

ALICE: Who are you?

MENSCHE: I am looking back.

ALICE: That figures.

MENSCHE: Christine Appleyard.

ALICE: Who is she? Have you seen her in time?

Another fiction from my good self.

MENSCHE : Not since Shrove Tuesday, July 5th 1856.

ALICE: Are you building her?

PETER: 1856? When was that?

MENSCHE: She is building herself.

PETER: Where?

MENSCHE: Here and now.

PETER: That doesn't make sense.

MENSCHE: I am glad you noticed.

ALICE: July 25th 1856 was not a Shrove Tuesday.

MENSCHE: I don't like facts. I go for fantasies. They tell me a lot more.

ALICE: Quite an amusing principle.

MENSCHE: It's nice to be appreciated.

ALICE: I am beginning to understand.

MENSCHE: That's good. You are doing better than I am.

PETER: This man is a joker.

ALICE: (*looks hard at MENSCHE*) Excuse me. A cannibal tale has just come in.

MENSCHE: A what?

ALICE: A new story. I am in the old Myford Lathe factory now. Beeston. The two Nazi radio beacons crossed overhead. Phil Cohen has just met Dot.

PETER: (*looking hard at MENSCHE*) This man is a clown.

MENSCHE: What beams?

ALICE: Guiding the pathfinder Heinkels of KG100. They tried to get to Chilwell Ordnance Depot. Night of the 14th April 1942. Do you still misunderstand?

MENSCHE: Not half.

PETER: (*looks hard at MENSCHE*) This man is a joker.

ALICE: I've lost Chilwell Depot. I can't sustain that far back yet. I am having to manufacture. The images are slow, drifting. Bad resolution.

PETER: (*looks hard at MENSCHE*) This man is unreal.

ALICE: That is virtual information.

PETER: Dream-leak?

ALICE: No, that's different. Wait. Where are you now?

PETER: Do you mean in time?

ALICE: Who am I tonight?

MENSCHE: A very good question. Who are you whenever?

ALICE: Tonight I am cities

MENSCHE: Well that must be very nice for you.

Like the old-style *News of the World* reporter, I got up and said I had to leave now. Dr. Deborah took me by the arm. Perhaps she knew that her touch cancelled any thought of leaving that I might have. A warning voice inside me said that this was far too nice a feeling on a first acquaintance.

"Did you enjoy that dialogue?"

"Almost. What was that about cities?"

"That's her switch-on code. She changes state when she hears it. That's how the Rogue language works. We call it *swarm*. The grammar is image-association based."

Swarm? That was the word Portcullis used. Portcullis, like Deborah, like mummy indeed, was everywhere

Her laughter chilled my bones. I was in thrall.

"What was that historical bit? She was talking about a guide beam for Nazi Blitz bombers. How did she get that hard information? And why are your bots so interested in my face?"

"In a pure media system a face and general appearance are the only things they have to go on."

"They must feel well deprived."

"They're downloading all your past destinies if you like. Like myself, you have been countless people. They will decode every crease, every fold. It's all just just information processing. Perhaps you once fished from a boat on the Volga in 1700. They'll find you there."

Her statement was even more chilling than her laughter.

"You have to bear in mind that these creations reason in terms of pure visual media images. They are essentially non-cerebral systems, although sometimes the little tricksters try not to appear as such at times. As any good artist will tell you, a face is built of an infinite series of layers upon layers. Each element belongs to the past, a life you have lived and a death you have suffered. The Rogues can unwrap a face, look at it as a complex of masks, shows, and performances that make up a person. They don't see atoms or molecules. They see perhaps who you were before you were born. That, you'll agree, is much more important. It's like looking at a very long series of tree-rings which make up a person. It's a lot better than DNA. They can see the dramas, the loves, the hates and the intrigues of the faces that make up your particular face. It does not yet come through complete, of course."

"Thank the gods for that."

"It comes through in bits and pieces, like the Blitz bomber. Forget rigidity. Media consists of infinite fields. Forget facts, system states are GO."

She smiled, terrorising me again.

"What's a field?"

I sounded like a lamb's last bleat before the slaughter.

"If X, who has never ever known or been near Y, nevertheless looks like Y, that's the field. Forget about spatial distance. Shape-families form such a field. Spatial separation is utterly meaningless in this context. The Rogues use nothing but common pictographs as reasoning. Some people call it JPEG Grammar."

I watched the previously naked Rogue blonde now carefully dress herself as Dr. Deborah took a phone call.

The non-Rogue phone conversation was intriguing.

"What? Don't be stupid. Fuck off, you Left Liberal little turd. Go and have a wank to the *Guardian* Arts Supplement or something. No, you can't come here. You'd never get through."

She then spoke in very rapid Hebrew, which she did not know I understood. It was too comically obscene to reproduce.

"We're finished. Oiled gulls, dead sea, polluted skies. Radiation cancer clusters. Bye bye. Get a life."

"Who was that?"

"The outgoing."

"Boyfriend?"

"Yes. The future is nigger."

Portcullis again. I was a dead white man.

"There goes one sad goy. Dead white man."

Wow! The target reflections were coming in thick and fast.

"Dead white science. Fuck him."

"You're a hard woman."

"Not really. For his sins he's a bog-standard conventional scientific hooker. Very much Old Science. Top plasma physicist at twenty two, and all that. Mechanist. Yuk. None of these young Victorian Station Masters have discovered Media yet. They're still computational. They're still looking for rigid connections between things. Frankly, I'd rather eat my shorts. Now listen to me carefully."

"Yes ma'am."

"I have created nothing more or less than Story Technology. Dorothy, that girl you were so intrigued with just now, is an example of such reasoning. She understands story-*states*, not physical *directions*. Rogues reason *imagistically*. Nothing in their head is linear. They swarm and absorb, like an infinite sponge. There are no pathways from say, k to f in such a Rogue hive. There is no time between change of state a to state b. Futhermore, when Rogue X gets experience Y, the same experience is felt instantaneously by all Rogues of type X."

"Dorothy is now making up her face, combing her hair. Aren't these directions?"

"They're simulated directions. Without such things they could not talk to the external world."

"Do they fight?"

"They compete. They have target audiences, not enemies. They see rival commodities, not foes. Antagonists as we know them cannot be defined in the Rogue world. Everything is performance, theatre. As I keep telling people, reasoning is as much about style as is an old Victorian slide-rule."

She emphasised the last word. I was not only out of date, I was out of my depth in many more ways than one. Concepts came big in this place. Whilst I was absorbing the idea of infinite sponges and stylistic Victorian slide-rules, the stout Dr. Deborah took another call to some hapless enquirer.

"No. Science is now wet and soft. Get your girders out of my fucking life, will, you? And stuff your weights and measures and your rules and regulations world up your arse, right? Goodbye."

"Is that the incoming monkey?"

"No, just another young hopeless prick from the Isaac Newton Institute in Cambridge. They're always ringing up here asking stupid questions about computation. Bloody Flatlanders."

There it was again. My mother's word, riding through the cosmos.

"You know — 'is this connected to that, and is that connected to this?' Like boy scouts in a Victorian telephone exchange. Trying to work out how the world works step by step. Counters of sand grains, that's what I call them. They think only measurement is real, you know? None of these so-called scientists have reached cyber yet. Just as Isaac Newton did't know about electricity, these scientists don't know about the image-based universe. Most of them think TV is just something to keep the kids quiet. Pain in the arse."

3. Meet Thelma Smith

Dr. Deborah now led to me to what I can only call a self-service cafeteria. Here were many ordinary-looking Rogues apparently doing such ordinary things as selecting food, carrying their trays to tables, eating, and talking with what appeared to be groups of friends.

"The food looks good."

"It isn't. It is what some Rogues call *shuvolla*. This is an odourless paste we had made up for advanced Rogues who have started to grow minimal excretory and urinal systems. It also provides energy."

"You've got to be kidding."

"That's nano for you."

"It sounds like something off the back of a Mars Bar wrapper."

"You are in the right area, sir!"

Still laughing, she now led me to another room in which there were Rogues improvising two- and three-part dialogues. Other groups were swordfencing, doing gymnastics, and group script-reading.

"This is the Rehearsal Room. This is where we make science into pure rock'n'roll."

"Do they have duties?"

I was flogged out. My imagination was gone. I sounded like a Flatlands vicar asking for better behaviour in the Girl Guides changing rooms. I was well and truly lost.

"The secret of intelligence is play. Try to direct too strongly, and the system gives you all the wrong answers."

"They just waste time?"

A haughty toss of her long black locks was her response. I tried to hide a blush by putting my hand across my face and pretending to scratch my brow. By this time I was completely gone. Just one look at her heaving chest put my feet at the back of my head.

"The secret of studying what we call intelligence is to allow systems to play. Impose order, and systems won't talk. Only media allows this condition fully. Conventional scientists take little notice of media, and even less notice of play and misbehaviour. Science has almost nothing to say about humour, anomalies, even less about human relationships. They make simplistic cartoon distinctions between fact and fiction and they call it reality. For them the world of appearances is intact. Doctors cure, policemen arrest criminals. Good behaviour means health. Lies mean criminality, death and disease."

As she spoke, her magnificent chest became twin Arks of the Covenant. I loosened my collar as she spoke.

"I dispensed with all these fixed reference frames. I conceived of the brain as a multimedia mix, and gave Artificial Intelligence limitless imagination, as it were. The first generation of nano engineering gave me the body-tools. I created the first mini-Rogues over twelve years ago with Robert Fallon, who created the flubber bodies from nano-weave."

"Wait. You're going too fast. You mean this whole thing was kept from the public for twelve years?"

"We operated on a very small scale at first, of course. The problem was..."

She almost bit her lip as if I had somehow persuaded her to say too much. For a moment she looked rather sad. I don't think she had been out in the world for a very long time. The idea occurred to me that perhaps I was the first piece of ordinary human crap she had related to for years.

"That a few escaped. We'd never anticipated a security problem. That hindered our funding for quite some time. This first group of escapees formed a small community in the suburbs of Newcastle, where they got up to all kinds of tricks. They were broken up as a terrorist band by police in 2000, in a WACO-type operation. We managed to keep at least most of the important details of this incident from the public."

Lowering her voice, she pointed out discreetly a young woman in her early twenties a couple of tables away.

She was calmly slicing a wedge of what looked like apple pie.

"That is Thelma Smith. She's a MK-3*, one of our most advanced models. She was in a batch of FREAK 2s rescued by radical activists in 2001. She was recaptured by Government Labs Contract Agents and released as SSPPCs (SAFE, or Self-Programmable Prototypal Citizens). She is officially Registered as Thelma Smith at Social Security, Westbourne Grove, Notting Hill.

"She was an early escapee, but she was found by a music producer singing in the Salvation Army Hall, Portobello Road."

"Do you know Portcullis Maid Marian, the rock singer?"

"Vaguely."

"Is she a Rogue?"

"We wouldn't know."

"Don't you keep a list of the damned things — er — I mean people, I mean folk? Aren't they testable?"

"Of course. But they create and manage all kinds of changes within themselves: appearance, character, everthing. As far as managing them and testing are concerned, we can't do much because the Public Rogues (as we call them) are all surrounded by shysters from the Transhuman Lawyers Association. You should see what they are throwing at us. We get hit by rocks from Civil Rights to the UN Charter. I tell you every single left-liberal bollock-brain is after us. As for the media mob, well you can imagine that, can't you? The great thing is that very few can get here given the state of the campus."

Distant explosions and gunshots made her point as she continued.

"And the postmen won't come here. That prevents me from receiving the boxes of noxious substances that are addressed to me personally.

"What about the naked pictures of your good self? They're all over the planet and the Web."

"That's outgoing mail."

"Really?"

"I have them printed. Prevents people seeing scientists as acne-ridden nerds with bad teeth and thick spectacles who torture animals to death."

"Let me ask you a question. Some say Portcullis wasn't born of natural parents. They say she just sprang up fully-formed one night in The Groucho Club."

"I remember. Entertainment plasma, that's what The Guardian called it. The Telegraph weighed in by calling Portcullis the first example of a non-carbon-based life form"

"She wasn't one of your early experimental escapees, was she?"

"Could be an offspring."

"An offspring?"

"Even alien."

"What?"

"I have to tell you something. There are now people in this business other than myself."

"I knew it."

"We can recognise my own Rogues most times by singular characteristics. We knew it was Thelma in the Salvation Army Hall because the Police had been told that she was forever singing songs from musical shows of the 1930s and did not need sleep. Most of the very first Rogue generation were easy to catch in this respect. The majority were far too obviously over-specialised to evade detection."

"You didn't get them all back?"

"You see, as I said, these first experiments were far too successful, quite beyond our wildest dreams. The ones we could not catch were the ones who quickly learned how to change and develop new roles and specialisations. They learned also how to feign sleep and even grow (yes!) primitive excretory and reproduction organs."

"I can't believe that."

"Get rid of old bio-cells and anything can be done. It's all about information, not atoms. Provided the information is there and provided it can be processed and directed, an entire and complete being can be manufactured somewhat independent of the usual environmental resources. The nano-meme is the new cell. Forget old biology."

"I'm frightened."

"Oh don't worry, they're harmless."

"I'm talking about you."

"Oh don't worry, I'm just an experimenter."

"That's what I mean."

She looked puzzled. She had not been out in the common world for a long time, and had not much notion of threat. I let her off the hook.

"Tell me more about Thelma."

"Thelma can now just about pass muster as Consumer Life Level 3. Talking to her would only indicate perhaps a slightly odd or eccentric person who would certainly pass without much comment in the average crowd. She now has natural functions; prior to that she excreted an odourless green nano-paste through her fingertips."

"Love to have been there when she felt the urge."

"At first we made a mistake in writing her off as a harmless and primitive Category 1 *Rogue*. This caused her to suffer catastrophic image schizophrenia before her rock band had a series of hits. That put Thelma in the world spotlight until she panicked and ran back to us."

"What was wrong with her?"

"Icon dementia. It could have happened to your Portcullis."

"Sounds better than a bent nail in the eye."

"You see, talking to too many cartoons at one time can result in a kind of media diabetic condition. The images fail to secrete enough new shows to balance themselves. The result is a kind of green blooming pond algae in the brain consisting of old acts *ad infinitum*. Forget afflicted biocells. It's old jokes that are Thelma's problem."

"She tells old jokes?"

"Very old."

"Like about stage coaches and swords?"

"And far older than that."

"What, cave painting and woolly mammoths?"

"Yes."

I used my best Cockney accent to stifle my rising hysteria. "Cor blimey, Deborah, stone the crows."

She laughed out loud, and the warning voice inside me came back again. I was beginning to more than like the cut of her jib. Again her voice came from afar.

"Using Thelma as subject, we initiated an experimental investigation into illness as a function of viewing concentrate. This condition can result in total collapse of the consumer expectation chains within the internal ecology of channel-options. As can be seen, she is stressed out through lack of metaphor. Her media landscapes have decayed, note her dated clobber, which went out with Frankie Avalon or *The Supremes*. She is at the moment undergoing a crisis. She is locked into style-loops and we can't get her out of those at the moment."

Thelma bit a nail, glanced in our direction, and quickly looked away.

"As I said, she passes muster in human company, but can only talk about *I Love Lucy* DVDs and how to organise her extensive viewing archives of that period. Her vulnerability is too much Retro culture. Suggestions have been made she should rationalise the management of her Prime Times of the distant past."

Been there, done that, but not this, I thought to myself.

"After Rock Scaramouch went to jail in the US for raping Thelma, she became full of media-survivor guilt, and somehow lost her wired-in cut-and-paste viewing objectives. At present she is undergoing image-information upgrade. Still has some PP (Perverse Preoccupation) with low-IQ head-games of the distant TV analogue past, but this can happen to such a style leader as Thelma, who has been adored by thousands. It's the result of getting confused between stars of several very distant eras at once, and not being able to tell one performance from another. Our soap-schedule therapy usually cures this problem of having too many screens in the viewing head at once.

"She's still apt to give warnings of bygone air raids in the middle of solo music spots. On one occasion she warned of the approach of a German World War I *Zeppelin* raid in the middle of singing her hit song *Theological Improvisation*. This of course made her famous beyond compare. But she lives uneasily with fame, does Thelma. She has tried to re-invent herself several times by creating powerful images of what she calls her barbaric ancestry."

At that moment a 1,000 watt *muezzin* rang out from the mosque above.

"Judging by that campus out there, the barbarians are at the door. Listen to the bastards."

"We get this all day. I'm thinking of getting a Ram's horn for Rosh Hashanah and giving them some competition. This is just one of the reasons why we're moving the entire project to a secret destination. That's why most Rogues you see here are tranquillised."

"How you do that?"

"Lock them into a single soap-loop. They can't escape unless they have the algorithm. Some of the super-clever models have tried to get it by foul means or fair, but they have not yet succeeded."

"You've lost me."

"Best way to show you what's happening to her head right now is to show you the lyrics from her current rap hit."

Taking a sheet of paper from her briefcase, Deborah read out aloud.

"'Get yourself a new set of stars and personalities and recompose the Past. Rehearse, re-script. Get a new meme. It's old schmaltz that causes illness. Don't bother with atoms, cells or molecules, transcend! Become art form, like Freddy Mercury, like scientific Ufology, and leather nuns. You know it makes sense. Facts went out with the last jailhouse fag tanks. It's showtime, so blast your wronged liver with a personality. Let the stars take on your illness. Out-perform disaster, out-style illness. Flush out your old metaphors, and boogie on!'

"That put her to Number One in eighteen charts worldwide.

"She's had other moments of fame. On Reality TV, Thelma once upped her shift, climbed a camera stanchion and promptly emptied a terrifying flush of yellowish liquid nano over leading personalities of Media Nation. According to some ruthless comedians in the Press, the lower nation closed its eyes and gave a silent prayer of thanksgiving."

"Now tell me. What the hell are they made of?"

"The bodies are super-flubber. The minds are formed of mass suggestion bacillus, woven by viewing schedules alone. My mind elements have been called Rumford Nano Viral Sculptures."

"No molecules?"

"No. Just media. Suggestions. Just a little bio-stuff for sustenance and options, but otherwise, just images. The only way to control Thelma, for example, is by threat of image-withdrawal of certain leading media-personalities who act as image-keys from certain performance-eras. This is New Science: Media is a new Realm of Matter. That's the thesis that got me Nobel in 1998."

"And no food intake?"

"They simulate it. We are working on actual intake. The latest models can simulate almost anything if needs be. Electrical energy is all they need. They generate it by body motion and solar panels. They are self-repairing. Crushing, fire, doesn't matter with the Rogues. They just re-clone from an image formula."

"And breeding?"

"I have told you, I am not allowed to say anything more about that."

"There's a lot of things you can't say anything about."

"We don't know everything about what goes off inside their heads."

"Not an inspiring answer."
"We're in free fall here. We have launched, we are travelling."
"But you don't know quite where?"
"No."

4. The Fascination

A tall, young, rather muscular man now joined Thelma at her table. Both waved merrily to Deborah, who waved back. I took note of the food they were given, feeling sure it was the famed *shuvolla*. I hoped the ham sandwich put in front of me by a Stepford-type waitress was what the old world called *real*. I bit deep in order to prevent chronic disorientation as Dr. Deborah spoke in hushed tones.

"The man who has just joined Thelma at her table is Cyril Fish. He is a Cone Head Type Z, Self-Regulating MK 5. Scientific type. Very advanced. Now manages to eat and defecate. Such advances take a long time. Large-scale adjustment can be difficult. Cyril eats semi-liquidised *Hartley's Kipper-Twats* by the barrel, and drinks *Manfred's Double Dream Topping* by the firkin. Has equivalent trouble with money-systems. He tries to deal in *double-doubloons*, Roosevelt *Dimes*, early Napoleonic *centesimi*, and forged 1943 Mussolini *lira*, though where he gets some of these from is a mystery.

He also gets confused by the time of day. The trouble is that as a Freezone Type IV, he's likely to turn up in the small hours ringing doorbells and delivering mercifully brief lectures on Michael Faraday's family. Lives in several historical eras simultaneously, with encyclopaedic knowledge of each period still living and developing as if time had no effect. He has been known to speak eight languages, both ancient and modern. Looks like a normal male, quite attractive, and he even has normal sexual functions, but tends to recite parts of the United States Constitution just before the point of no return."

Before I could think of a suitable reply to that, from somewhere deep in the recesses of the building I now heard what sounded like fire alarm bells. A Mickey Mouse theme song pealed from her mobile.

"Excuse me, there's been a bomb scare. My team will have to go to the shelters."

She touched my hand. Again. "Come next week George, and I'll tell you more."

Despite the word "George" ringing pleasantly in my head of a sudden, I was glad to leave. Several of the *Rogues* had eyed my *Bangladeshi* computer, which Thelma, laughing, pointed out to other Rogues, who chuckled in turn. This was strange because Deborah, quite astonished, said that this reaction was a very rare example of collective Rogue-focused group humour she had ever seen. This was only the second time — the first being the Max Bygraves fiasco. A smiling Rogue Dorothy (now fully dressed), reached out to touch my *Bangladeshi*, but smiling back, I politely moved the instrument away, fearing another loss.

When Deborah Rumford saw the object of Dorothy's attention, she handed me a *Tesco* carrier bag to shroud the universally despised apparatus. I was grateful for this, since the DSS would only renew the dread beasts three times (aware of the social difficulties), and I was on my third issue. After the third loss, the DSS gave a *zec* vouchers for Internet cafes, not to my taste at all.

With her voice echoing "George" in my head, and her touch still on my hand, I tucked my Tesco bag under my arm and headed back to the Tabernacle to write my feature.

I found concentration difficult. I kept seeing her face, kept wondering what she was doing. I was in a universally recognised state. I was once warned by an ancient hippy that summer in Powis Square could be a heavy number.

Once home the situation became embarrassing. If I started a sentence about a box of matches, somehow Deborah's name crept in, to great amusement all round.

To show the state I was in, I pinned up the *RaveClit* picture of Deborah Rumford in a skimpy black basque. The girls started giggling and nudging one another. I took it down, but the girls found yet another, pinned it up and giggled some more. Even the *Manang* gave a sly knowing smile as she prepared dinner. I am sorry to say that I blushed all the way through the meal and blamed it on the curry, which raised yet more laughter.

"He's hooked."

Said Svetlana.

"Fucked, more like."

Said Betty.

"Happy hunting. Nice to see you; to see you, nice."

Said the *Manang*, whose perverted English was improving.

twelve

The Wormwood Scrubs Affair

1. The Web Meme Opens

I SPENT the next week preparing my report on the Rumford Rogues, and for once I wrote it myself without any help. Of course I had to live through many cracks about it, such as "takes a woman to put a man to work," etc., but for once Price was pleased, and he ran the Rogue story almost immediately.

All hell was let loose. Price's ego now knew no bounds as international Press, Radio, and TV interest grew by the hour. The trouble was that Deborah would only talk to me. This made *The Brentford Sceptic* the only source of live information about the Rumford Rogues. "Mensche, I want you to grab this Deborah Rumford and make her the star of *The Brentford Sceptic*. When are you seeing her again?"

"She's disappeared, gone to ground apparently. I can't get her on the phone. I am told the lab is now sealed for some reason. In that area she could be dead, murdered. We don't know."

"Keep trying."

"It could be weeks before we have a follow-up. I want you to get out there and keep up the momentum."

That sounded ominous. Another day, another job.

"What's that? Remember, I am new to labour."

"Not now you aren't. I've been told that you are hooked. The Viewers in *The Ape and Parcel* are impressed."

He gave me a wink and a nod.

"I have heard that the attraction is mutual. But a woman like Deborah can be expensive. Can you keep her in the manner to which she is accustomed?"

"I am an aristocrat. Money is irrelevant."

"Well, what I have in mind for you is a truly aristocratic task. This will impress the good Dr. Deborah far beyond riches, believe me."

I held my breath. Couldn't wait to hear what Price's idea of a class act was.

"I want you to do a full report on the mysterious crop circles. Thanks to you and the Rumford Rogues, we now have a new young audience."

For once he had me. I had always been interested in the strange circles which appeared every summer in crop fields. To my mind, they were cut with technical precision, as if machine-made. Most appeared overnight, displaying elaborate designs. Except in the most obvious cases, there were few signs of any disturbances in the crop by would-be makers, and no one reported teams of pranksters arriving or departing.

The system was far too clean for my liking.

Since there were few leaks, rumours, or betrayals, I thought I might start by making a few of these things myself and see what happened. Perhaps in this way the circle system could be talked to, to use Dr. Deborah's phrase.

I didn't leave the Tabernacle for days, thinking about the problem. Finally, I decided that the best thing to do would be to create a Web Meme using my own version of some of Dr. Deborah's ideas.

2. Ropes and Planks

First I made up a website and claimed to be the maker of a well-known and rather spectacular crop circle. Immediately, severely depressed Nessie-gnomes from the *Fortean Times* (a kind of English hermitage), responded savagely. They were followed by nail-biting sceptics, the last few hippies, and hundreds of New Age occult camp followers of all kinds who had been raving about this circle for months. Such elaborate formations in ripening crops were attributed to many things. The accusations ranged from UFOs to witchcraft to trickster-doings of crop-gods of the ancient world. There were even assertions that Bob and Doug, two retired radio presenters, worked the patterns with ropes and planks whilst they were blind drunk.

This crowd was what I supposed Deborah would call a *cyber-swarm*. As she had said, the mechanics of a massless Swarm are entirely different to the conventional algebraic geometry of lines and nets of railways, telephones and telegraphs, water systems, and postal services. As distinct from a machine, a web Swarm had no physical existence. It was pure cyber, but rang in the head-webs like a bathroom sponge made of bell metal. One address meant every address. This was instantaneous posting to everybody. It was Christmas all year round, with no moving parts. Hit Mr. Brown, all Mr. Browns felt the blow instantaneously.

In thinking these thoughts, Deborah was always near. She was time, science, summer, all rolling in my head like a trawler in a heavy swell.

Svetlana and Betty were enthusiastic about my idea of a *cyber-swarm* as I outlined it. We got together a good operational team, and formed careful plans. We decided to "draw," as it were, some basic occult symbols, mixed with a few hieroglyphics, which we copied from a book.

When we were ready, we nipped out one evening to Wormwood Scrubs with a set of short planks and lengths of rope. My team consisted of Betty, Svetlana, plus Lucy and Dana, two young nubile Viewers from *The Ape*. The inclusion of this latter pair of Essex WAGS (said by Betty to be the biggest ranting gossips in the South of England) ensured the immediate spread of spectacular rumours, scandals, misrepresentations and plain lies. The DSS gave us a grant for some extra RAM for our *Bangladeshi,* which was most useful. This enabled us to inject some really wild blog ravings, which wound up the cyber-swarm to unprecedented heights of agitation.

We made one really good circle in the grass of the Scrubs, just outside the famous jail, which was quite dark when we first arrived. I positioned my team to make sure that we were observed by both passing traffic and many curious prisoners in Wormwood Scrubs jail, who operate the best bush telegraph in the world, despite being incarcerated.

Svetlana, Lucy and Dana wore yellow luminous micro-skirts and were bare-breasted. Myself and Betty wore nothing at all except devil masks, thus ensuring that our activity was somewhat well observed. We also concealed three burly minders in a nearby ditch in case any passers-by got out of order.

By the time we'd finished, the darkened prison was aglow with light, and shouts of somewhat savage encouragement were heard from its barred windows and ramparts. A curious crowd gathered almost immediately, and many photo-flashes fired, both from a gathering crowd and the prison. After a couple of hours, two tired bored constables arrived, but showed no interest as we'd made sure we weren't contravening any by-laws by doing what we were doing.

The circle was made, and after a few glasses of *Tree Frog* in *The Ape*, Lucy and Dana were carried off prostrate by two famous footballer boys, which ensured great media publicity all round. We three all got home pleased and excited enough to screw all night. This was much to the annoyance of Warden Sproat who, banging on the door, announced he would make a Full Report on the morrow, concerning incestuous paedophilia and child rape.

2. The Swarm

In the days that followed, using the extra RAM in our Bangladeshi, we wound up the Swarm (our nest of fuming Web blogs) into yet another superb frenzy, and left this nice mess of referential infinity on the back-burner for a week. Svetlana told me that in classical alchemy this stage is called *nigredo*, or basic substance. Betty then suggested we tell the mechanical *truth*, adding that this was always a vital element in any scheme of classical imposture, absolutely guaranteed to raise some equally classy denials and explanations.

Despite my somewhat pathetic democratic protests (I was never very good at democracy), yours truly was quickly located as the would-be leader of the team responsible for the Scrubs circle.

Absolutely delighted, Price read from *Last Days* magazine:

"Everyone knows in their heart of hearts that they live in a clapboard structure as phoney as an Obama smile or a Pentagon denial. I do of course appreciate that people want to get some sleep at night, and they can only do that when the mysterious 20,000-mph right-angled turns that are recorded on radar are transformed into migrating crows."

With such publicity, my life started to get interesting. After I weathered the first set of screaming counter-denials from the *cyber-swarm*, highly intelligent serial killers wrote to me from the best jails in Britain. With their help and advice, I prepared what the *Daily Express* called a masterstroke, or what some cyber theoreticians called a counter-hoax.

I claimed that my Scrubs Circle was not made by myself, or any party associated with myself. As a metaphysical bonus I apologised for any hurt inflicted through such silliness, and apologised for my mischievous mendacity.

This retraction caused a fresh storm of controversy, within the *cyber-swarm* and without. The "scientific" crowd weighed in with an "explanation" as wondrous as the sun and moon. They claimed that our circle was made by the peculiar mating patterns of herons, of which there was a family nesting on the banks of the local canal nearby. Another sceptical rationalist "scientific" heroine claimed that my Scrubs Circle was the result of weather abnormalities caused by "spurious" emanations from lighthouses, the nearest of which was at least 100 miles away.

I exercised great patience. I was on my way. Writs of various kinds arrived. I acquired a stalker, always a sign of coming fame. Humourless and near-suicidal manic-depressives from the *Sceptical Enquirer* said I should be hung, drawn and quartered, and my head put on a pole on Tower Hill.

Things were happening very quickly. The Tabernacle was under siege.

Meantime, the BBC, still after the talents of both Svetlana and Betty, hoped to resurrect them as "personalities," if only because their names were in the headlines. Consequently, Svetlana was whipped away by the BBC producers, and her *Dictionary of Truth* programme became a national riot. They gave her a TV series. Now she sent me food parcels from her new place in Camden. In turn, Betty was at Number One in the charts with her band, MothTown Skankers. She sent me food parcels from her new big loft in St. John's Wood.

The result was that what with the press and national media milking both the Rumford Rogues and cyber-swarm stories, I now had only the Manang to protect me against the paparazzi and a flyblown miasma of media types, flailing drunks and crack-driven choirboys. Her thrown bricks and her short Saipan fish-harpoon sufficed to keep onlookers at bay and preserve within my small capsule in the Module some degree of meditative silence.

With my name in the headlines, the DSS started to press me for an account of what they called my *condition.*

I repeated what I had told them throughout the years: I was a gentleman in permanent distress. As a concept this did not go down well with the multi-ethnic multicultural one-syllable Flatland social workers, who had never heard of a thing called a gentleman, never mind servants. I told our New Citizens (almost all of whom hailed from beyond Calais) that I had only one unpaid staff, and she fed off the under-subsidised scraps from my table. These baffled clerks (whose English was limited to TV-pidgin) going to and fro in the midst of this speculation became national entertainment for a while. I was lampooned, cartooned, ridiculed; I was praised, even deified and worshipped by a team of chanting black women in embroidered nightshirts.

Thus began a whole series of media and urban legends in themselves. It was of course found out very quickly that I was an authentic claimant to the Scottish throne. Others claimed that I was a lost extraterrestrial alien, or fallen god. For many weeks, outside broadcast units were parked night and day in front of the Tabernacle. Celebrated "personalities" tried to interview me. The ancient Flatland bisexual crones who wrote "literary" novels were always the worst. All from Fitzrovia, they wore woolly jumpers and looked like Heinrich Himmler in a bad temper. The men from the same area were worse. Most were sixty-year-old neo-Edwardian public school prefects whose Gay Pride badges sat like pouting anuses upon their lapels. Both sexes became nervous, pale-faced and showed buck-teeth when I deliberately slipped in the word "technology."

Of course as soon as it became known that, genetically speaking, I was a top nob, the camp effete crew from the A&F also made a beeline for yours truly. Seeing their elongated vowels bent back into pure Essex-speak after making their way through cursing junkies, speed-ballers, and dazzle-eyed crackheads was a great delight, and provided much entertainment in the Tabernacle. There were much more interesting exchanges with considerably less enlightened individuals.

thirteen

A Visit from the Taliban

IT WAS about this time that I had a visit from Dr. Shadrak, my out-sourced DSS worker. A nice friendly man, genuine Taliban-British from Henley on Thames, he was the image of Aboo-Derby, the President of Iran (I can never spell or pronounce his name).

Dr. Shadrak was what was called a Unique Needs Social Worker, and his PhD came from the same mystic regions where dwelt Bin Laden.

Prior to his arrival in this Sceptred Isle, he'd been a leading ambush expert against NATO forces in Afghanistan. His notorious DSS 'Introductory Pamphlet' (which made the front page of *The Sun*), stated that he decided to come to Britain because he needed a new set of free dentures and some equally free treatment for his many bullet and shrapnel wounds. He was promptly given a mansion in Hampstead whose previous British owner had committed suicide through bankruptcy. In addition to a job, he was also handed £3,000 a week in benefits for his eight children and three wives. Dr. Shadrak told *The Sun* that he intended to go back to his "native obligations" which entailed blowing up British soldiers.

Imagine the quite unique scene of this visitation. I myself now had two famous wives, both of whom had their own TV programmes. I myself was famous because of the Scrubs circle business, and of course the Rumford Rogues. In addition, Shadrak's face was on the front of every popular newspaper, if only because his eldest daughter was a Soho pole dancer.

The result? The Tabernacle was surrounded by the global media. The Presenters were all quite astonished and amused that I was in receipt of Social Security, and they all dutifully ignored Shadrak's history as an unrepentant Muslim bomber-stroke-British Social Worker.

The *Manang* and myself were surrounded day and night by broadcast vans, and the parking situation was not improved by the regular visits of Svetlana and Betty in their newly-acquired stretch limousines. The food parcels they brought me were another source of media astonishment. One or other, or both, would occasionally stay the night, and this stirred wonderfully the pots of speculation. Journalistic investigations into both my super-marital status and Dr. Shadrak's PhD in 'agriculture' began, and weekly instalments were published of the progress.

Even high consumer-end intellectuals (British Left-liberal standard, that is) from the new 'workshop' universities began to take interest in what they called the Tabernacle's 'multiplex situation'.

With an armful of fearsome docketry, Dr. Shadrak blithely made his way through the lighting and the technology, He interviewed me in thick Manchester-Afghani, with a touch of Anglicised Bollywood. Do bear in mind that every syllable went straight up to the satellites and finished up in cortexes from Bangkok to Alaska and all points in between. What they made of some of it caused great speculation amongst the *glitterati*.

My entire life now entered more channels, nets, sites, and broadcasts than the Devil himself would ever have believed possible. Instant by instant, my life and being both were smeared over the planet, entering minds faster than you could say *Paradise Lost*. There was no OFF switch for me, or anybody else in my life. And since even *The Daily Express* said that I'd entered the unconscious, no-one could get rid of me any more than Marilyn Monroe, still alive and breeding in the head. The *Daily Mail* said that when I was long-pressed into coal seams, whatever beings existed would still gaze in wonder at what had happened at the Tabernacle.

This was all madness of course, but no more mad than Shadrak. After Afghanistan he was quite unfazed by the batteries of cameras and light he had just walked through to get to me.

"Mr. Mensche, I want to verify you, already."

"I'm not surprised."

"Where do you come from actually, please?"

"The Yellow Brick Road."

"Postcode if at all?"

"Forty fousand fevvers on a brush."

"Yellow what? I can't find that on the SatNav. Never mind. That's alright, please. Mr. Mensche, It says here you are an R/34xc29. That's a special category."

"What for, brother?"

His traffic-warden brow clouded. He frowned, scratched his head, and stood puzzled.

"It's something pencilled in here. It says *losers*. Which means you'll have to have a means test, already."

"Stool or sperm? Close the door and I'll draw the curtains. If the Day of Judgement should happen to arrive, explain things to the Messiah. He will understand the situation. You got the right Mandelson EuroSpecimen Containers in your bag there?"

"Are you micro-tagged yet?"

"No. I'm Low Life Profile MK4. The Index folk don't bother adjusting the advertisements for my psycho-social group. We Welfare heroes are specialised criminals. We don't need a tag. You can locate us anywhere, any time. We have surrendered. There is now a white flag sticking out from the arse of every true subsidised British Believer. It's the ultimate surrender."

"I've got no crimes listed here on these here dockets."

"We True Believers are guilty of imagining. It's a form of modern confession."

"That's not a crime, please."

"The crime is believing in everything. No need for stem cells, rationalisations, or regular viewing schedules. Surrender is the most wonderful experience. I cannot wait for the next stage of my social-scientific enlightenment."

"It says here you haven't done anything wrong,"

"Sir, I imagine. It is the greatest crime. I make images. I play God. In the bargain, I have the damnable cheek to think I am absolutely wonderful. That's the unforgivable sin within the spectrum of rationalised social evolution."

"This won't make any difference to your Benefit."

"As they told Christ on the Cross."

"Who is that, then?"

"Steady now. I wish to make a statement. 'Suspended between Africa, Arabia, and Queer Nation, I remain calm.' Have you got that down?"

"What was that third country?"

"Ask the Media."

"Are you from there?"

"Almost. In ten years' time, you'll be able to put a fist through me, and I won't notice."

"You look for work if at all?"

"I am looking for enlightenment. Pray for me."

"Did you get your Mental Disability Payment credit in your account early this week?"

"I got a piece of what England owes every Scot, if that's what you mean. They pay their debts by instalments."

"England? They lost against Turkmenistan Thursday night."

"They're as useless as I am, Shadrak."

"I've must to put down something about your general condition, yessir."

"I am in a condition of perpetual amazement. It's a modern state of innocence. My clothing allowance coupons alone give me an oceanic feel."

"I'll must to make a full report, please."

"Tell the beloved Authorities that I am designed to fail. It's called contra-Evolution. The beloved scientists have just discovered it. I am a new species, specifically designed not to progress or evolve."

The ambush eyes sparkled, the Taliban mouth gaped, and his fingers curved as if for the activator switch of an improvised Explosive Device.

"We will continue with your subsistence, innit?"

Shadrak went away happy, working his way past the cameras, ab-ba-dabbering along to his iPod, and shuffling official forms like a true member of the lower middle class. I last saw him fading into the weak and watery social-democratic sunlight, narrowly avoiding being run down by the local corporation recycling truck.

That this exchange went up to scores of satellites was a source of great satisfaction to every *zec* in the Tabernacle. I was toasted and a good all-night party ensued, in which the Pethers family gave a floor-show to be remembered. This concluded with a purloined monkey riding a dancing dog, together with a truly awesome strip tease from Betty's cousin Sharon of Ladbroke Grove.

fourteen

The Explanations Arrive

1. Mine Author Wrote Me

NEXT I LAUNCHED what *Soiled* magazine called a masterpiece of an explanation. Using the Web Swarm as a suggestion-bacillus, I quickly withdrew my denial claim and I said that indeed I did make the Scrubs circle, but I made it in the spirit of a creative landscape "artist."

The sighs of relief from parents and priests in particular could be heard around the globe. Particularly satisfying was the red-faced outrage from the "scientific" heron-and-lighthouse crowd.

The *Guardian* was well happy with a splendid Left-liberal explanation. All was revealed: I was an avant-garde landscape "action painter" who just wanted to see the wonder of the theories my complex deceptions might give rise to.

At a stroke, with this model explanation I was rendered harmless again and almost everyone was happy but the scientists who, due to lack of a proper education, had absolutely no idea of what I was talking about. Mothers and fathers wrote to me saying that, finally, they were so glad their sons and daughters had been gulled by my most superior kind of very clever entertainment.

The *Bollox* website proclaimed that this explanation of explanations was one of the finest illusions ever created. I quote:

"Mensche is not a con man any longer, a liar or even what the bourgeoisie call a "fantasist." He is an artist, that is, a favourite puppy dog of a favourite son. You can scratch his tummy as he rolls before the hearth fires of the proud families of England."

But still the sceptics remained suspicious of this pseudo-explanation of "artist." More scientists and rationalists arrived at the Scrubs site, all sounding like the piano music that used to accompany the silent films of Charlie Chaplin. This time, those flickering frames which in the past had produced "earthlights," distant lighthouses, and dancing pregnant frogs as explanations for the mysterious circles, produced a harpy who announced from *The Fortean Times* that my Scrubs circle had been made by rutting hedgehogs.

Price was euphoric. *The Brentford Sceptic* was being talked about all over the world. Over a Quorn *Mint Plasma Sausage* in the Brentford Leisure Centre Bingo Cafeteria, he read from *Non-Cerebral Systems* a much-respected Journal dedicated to TV and Media analysis. The front page announced MENSCHE IS A MEME, and the article claimed: "George Mensche has now reached the Star stage of the Cyber Embryo. *The Times* has called him a modern *shaman,* Madonna has plans to put him in her video, and Faber & Faber have been on the phone asking what the phrase *post-modern* means."

"Great Stuff, Mensche. Just think of all that money flowing towards your good self."

"Oh, I don't accept any payment."

"I beg your pardon?"

"I'm on the Dole."

"Haven't you signed off?"

"No. I want to make the State pay for its sins."

"Can I quote you?"

"It is a religious matter. Only through supporting me can they attain grace."

"No wonder they call you The New Explanation."

"It's old, it's Blood. I play my role. The State plays its own."

"Did you explain this to them at the time?"

"They've yet to come to terms with this kind of obligation. They have forgotten such an impossibility as I have produced. But, give them time. They will remember."

"Remember what?"

"How to shut their mouths and take orders."

"Divine Right?"

"No. Just Right."

"They'll kill you, of course."

"Impossible. I am now in Prime Time. Rending of the flesh is meaningless."

"Ridiculous."

"Exactly."

Meantime, the Media raved on.

I was plagued in particular by one Kirsty, a top A&F media woman. This clone of a *Thunderbirds* Flight Attendant accused me of being a complete impostor. I shot back that in her world in particular, the idea of such things as impostors (complete or incomplete) was meaningless.

Which went down fine all round in the morning press.

I added that now she was about to experience the double benefit of seeing almost false theories arise from possible falsehoods, sponsored in turn by almost certain falsehoods. Kirsty's chipmunk jaw dropped when I added that all this could lead to a calculus of falsehoods. Poor Kirsty didn't know what on earth I was talking about, and a few weeks later plummeted from Prime Time grace and retired at twenty nine to write pre-electric novels about Jeremy and Jill in Hampstead.

Price jumped with joy. My photo appeared on the cover of *Mojo* magazine. Violent and hysterical crowds in front of the Tabernacle had to be hauled back by police.

My prediction to Kay Burley on *Sky News* that the Joker would arrive just as certainly as moon followed sun resulted in world headlines. The media raved on. Who, or what, was the Joker?

2. Enter the Joker

I didn't have long to wait for the Joker to make his entrance. The Joker was the crop circle that was not made by any human being. Though this circle was as crude as a parrot's "good morning," this time there appeared no explanations — at all, from anywhere. This Joker Circle, as it was soon called, appeared almost instantaneously in front of several picnicking families on Scrubs Common on a sunny afternoon. The disturbed earth and grass (tinted a shade between orange and yellow) rapidly formed rough patterns which from the air appeared to reflect classical geometrical theories.

In mythological tradition, there were found no less than three strange bloodless dog mutilations nearby, and some fine UFO footage was caught by the picnicking families. *The Sun*, splashing the spectacular pictures right across its middle pages, shouted that I was a winner in the Great God-Game.

Price, quite off his head with commercial inspirations, read out loud to me from the magazine *Tumult Vector*:

> "*Mensche has created life! Not from a test-tube or a womb, but from the alchemical furnace of the varied spectrum of the mass expectancy created. When the sceptics call that psycho-social, don't get depressed! This means that the things we imagine do come about. That transforms sceptics into fellow-magicians — which of course, we always knew they were.*"

Now I sat back and watched my system clone itself as the many shades of my suggestion-bacillus grew plausible web-like worlds.

There was however, some opposition. This came in the main from that well-known Flatland hermitage, *The Fortean Times*. This last refuge of severely-damaged Anglo-Saxons was the last shelter in cultural time of Nessie-gnomes, crabbed Bohemians, and pre-electric hobbits straight out of E.M. Forster's novel *Howards End*.

Worse was to come from the country cousins of *Magonia* magazine, a raw-boned Stalinist-Protestant publication, if ever there was. This stencilled broadsheet, put together by stout Lutheran dullards, was notorious for denying any kind of magical, mystical, occult, paranormal effects and manifestations or indeed any kind of miraculous, holistic, transcendental, or anomalous effect.

I was told that in the past, this hand-duplicated flyer had caused many suicides through inducing what *Manic Years* magazine called "Protestant Hysteria," which it claimed was induced by something called "fear of fantasy." The magazine claimed also that there had been created a whole new medical syndrome termed *Sceptical Dementia*, caused (it claimed) by something called "fear of anomalies." The quarterly journal *Protestant Times* joined in the general fracass by commenting on the "psycho-social illness" caused by these mysterious things called "fantasies," which apparently was their favourite word, or so I was told. *Protestant Times* stated also that "miracles should be small, and not happen very often." This edifying recommendation caused me some sleepless nights whilst seeking the path of true philosophy.

Both Forteans and Magonians invited me to a meeting to discuss what they termed "facts versus fictions." Such were the frenzied arguments about something called the *real* that I had to be rescued by my ever-present team of bodyguards. I was rushed into the grounds of the Commonwealth Institute, where an obliging police helicopter crew hauled me up and out from the vengeance of what Meat Banana magazine called " the seething crustaceans of Lutheran England."

Had my helicopter been equipped with bombs and rockets, I could have wiped out at least 30% of the Left-Liberal Home Counties intelligentsia at a stroke, and nobody would have been any the wiser, except for the absence of a few effete voices at "literary" parties.

These thoughts of mine were interrupted by Price reading aloud from *Entertainment State*, a magazine dedicated to cooking and pornography:

> *"Now we know that if a belief system (which after all is merely a series of suggestions as regards possibilities) is powerfully advertised, it will produce a cloned life which mimics those self-deceptions, mock-explanations, and double-bluffs within the self, which we call thinking."*

"How's fame suiting you then, Mensche?"
"I'd rather be in Bolton on a black Monday."

"Don't worry you'll soo get used to it. I see you with a coke nose and two nymphettes sucking your nipples."

Laughter from the corridor as Price continued reading. "Just as we were all prepared to switch on a continuous loop of Eastenders right before we took the full bottle of aspirin, George Mensche arrived to save us. Through his skilful manipulation of fraud and deception as art form, Mensche has rediscovered theatre and media both as new states of Matter. And it was all done by advertising in that prime time called consciousness. As the great man himself observed, 'We have learned through my demonstration that the beloved concepts of truth and reality are scandalous and disreputable beyond all conception.'"

The phone interrupted, Price snatched it up and screamed: "Mensche, she's back!" He turned and rasped: "Deborah Rumford — she wants to see you, tomorrow, HQ, twelve noon sharp."

Price paid for two armed minders, and I travelled to the university in a special armoured saloon. Throughout my visit, though discreetly standing at a distance, my protection squad did not let me out of their sight.

fifteen

Who am I Tonight?

I'D BEEN TOLD that conditions in the campus of Brentford Garage University had worsened since I was last there, and that was bad enough. Now warring drug gangs infested the area, some equipped with machine guns and grenades, and it was said that Army patrols were in the area. During this time, the only "academic achievement" of the Garage University had been the launching of a *Doritos* advertisement into space. Prizes had been given for the strengthening of garden wheelbarrows, the design of wheelie-bins, and easy-access "cottaging" software for gay pensioners.

Everywhere there was some connection to homosexuality. These agendas were going into the cultural body like needles thrust desperately into a twitching corpse.

I was in late Athens or Rome.

I was neither dead nor alive.

The Rehearsal Room was dark, the Rest Rooms deserted. Men hurried by carrying furniture and equipment. Many had American accents. The lighting was dim, and the last few Rogues carried their own bags to special vans and lorries guarded by private security guards armed with M-16s. Men in white lab coats (also with American accents) were everywhere supervising the packing and loading of specialised equipment. I got the distinct impression that the Rumford project was much bigger than ever I'd thought. I saw also that personnel now ignored Deborah entirely, as if she were now no longer important or necessary to a scheme of things which had somehow overwhelmed her.

It was under these peculiar and disturbing conditions that I noted that she had aged somewhat. She had something of a despairing look about her, although her spirits rose when she waxed lyrical about the latest Rogue developments.

"I'm glad you came, George."

This came with an embrace and a kiss on the cheek which left my hormones somewhat active.

"The Rogues are coming out with a new texture, a more dense fabric, with all kinds of new and peculiar associations. It's a far deeper level of image-organisation than we've ever achieved. It's longer, deeper, even lyrical. They're beginning to infer, speculate, and experiment with remote viewing without being detected as non-human. These are brave new developments but due to the move we just haven't had time to check completely on the latest mutations. The few Rogues we did check show they're intellectually mutating, *hour by hour*. It's no less than the discovery of a vast new field of information transfer! Listen to this."

A DVD opened up showing Thelma talking to Peter.

"Who am I tonight?"

"Who are you whenever?"

"Tonight I am cities."

"Where?"

"Now a slow drift of storehouses. Faces of incredibly ancient women and cloud-forms, then these replaced by huge spare parts sheds, seemingly of infinite extent, containing universal catalogue inventories of objects, faces, combinations of situations. I get the impression that all and everything is frozen in mental ice before some summer of realisation comes. A number is called out, and a face or an aircraft or even a grandfather clock is woken for active service in some story-game of which I am never allowed to see the progress, start, or finish."

"What is there?"

"I am looking at a telephone exchange of intermodulating stories."

"That's good."

"I want to attract their attention. I want to become part of one of the stories, and be carried by trains, trucks and ships and planes through the oncoming horizons of all cities."

"Where are you now?"

"Now the cities are gone. Now I am a passive, powerless watcher over entire continents."

"What do you see?"

"I see a French woman."

"Which one?"

"Renee. 1943. Lyons. Nervous enquiries about times and events. Pre-Cambrian rivers, seas, hills and villages long before human dwellings were lit at night, all eliminating Renee's blue eyes, her seamed silk stockings of long ago, her string of onions. Now sea and women again. Golden fish swim against green gloom into sheer black. This dark gives now endless multitudinous shape-families: herd, species and type. I swim freely in an image-fluid of many dimensions, a picture-flux of vibrant intensity. An enamel leaf-cluster of young women's faces, with their hair in the fashion of the 1920s, bursts into a complete thematic display of the circular: rings, spheres: marbles, planets, stone circles and bicycle wheels of time past."

"Are you still there?"

"Yes. Stop. Now a store-packing department on overtime trying to meet a midnight deadline. The stories are shouting warning."

"Where are you now, Thelma?"

"I am almost there —"

"Where?"

"... Flying cargoes of image-streams succeeding one another, images like strobe-lights. A sense now of activation of emergency supply lines, re-fuelling, re-arming, all for resistance to something in a beyond I cannot see. Now stop. What? Now start. A hesitant continuation. Then slow, quivering pulsations. I understand. Taps on the shoulder, from something without a mouth. Now nervous hesitations as the shoals of pictures flutter, hesitant and confused."

"Are you becoming aware?"

"Perhaps. Something feels good. But now bad image-weather. Now the long crest of a mighty shudder. Colour intensity diminished. Speed of flow sluggish. Images languid, indeterminate, without depth, character, nuance. For the briefest instant a mass production of pigmy-clones.

"Something moving through the trees. Another story. Another mind. A cannibal tale. Disturbance. Sky-flutter and crack of dry foliage from distant simulated valleys down by the cartoon-rivers. Who is here? Who am I tonight?"

"That was a run of coherence."

"Thank you, Peter."

"I don't like it, Thelma."

"Why?"

"Such images mean trouble. Attack. Defence. War."

"You are far too well-adjusted. All thought is trouble."

"That's a matter of opinion."

"What is opinion?"

Deborah switched off the video and turned to me, her hand now in mine.

"See? More fluidity, longer sentences, wider vocabulary. What do you think?"

"You're moving too fast."

"Isn't that good?"

"Not if you want to live."

"I'm under threat."

"I bet you are."

"But you didn't answer my question. What do you think?"

"You're near."

"Near what?"

My reaction was to indulge in a little of the kind of illegal speculation that had ruined my life. No one was supposed to do this any more. Untrammelled, speculative thinking without any kind of rationale caused endless trouble, like involuntary levitation or the sudden twisting of metal into a right angle. Experience was supposed to be complete, uniform, consistent — and therefore miracles should be small and not happen very often. That way they could be swept under the carpet and the screen of the rational world was kept in place. Well, here are a few of the impossibilities I caught on a night of fire and rioting in the far distance, complete with wailing sirens and distant explosions.

Fires and searchlights across her face, gunshots from nearby. I saw and recognised Deborah. Berlin, 1923, or thereabouts: remote viewing is not very good at numerals. They appear as fuzzy icons on the frontiers of infinite uncertainty. I saw her Jewish face covered with blood, handcuffed to a lamppost with the old German imperial coat of arms on it, picked out in gold. I smelt tear gas. I saw Erhardt's armoured cars moving through the bloodstained snow along the Unter den Linden. A swoon, a scream. Then she was gone. *Nacht und Nebel*. No notice of whereabouts.

Amazing what you can do to break the lock of objective appearances. Get back to the subtexts. What she was saying, here and now, was the most minute tip of her. I saw her great grandmother. Sepia tints. University teacher in Leipzig, circa 1890. Science and Communism. The last Grand Illusions. The two were to become almost identical, wasting lives, continents and dreams.

And young bright-eyed Deborah had forgotten. As she played basketball, divorced a brainless tennis-playing idiot with three "scientific" degrees, she was not aware of the dramas she was living and indeed had lived. I supposed that occasionally she would put aside the noise of the day and think about *nostalgia mysterieux* as the surf of a limitless sea broke against the rocks that were keeping her sane. It was, I supposed, the same for many Jews. All of them were older than the rocks on which they sat.

"Leipzig, 1890. The apple garden."

I could go deeper, but that required time. The word *Leipzig* was sufficient. An axe cleaved Deborah from skull to toes. Gulps of air, eyes not daring to meet mine. Gone was the facts screen, bang down the river with the Rules and Regulations universe.

She spoke with her back to me, watching the fires outside the window as if I had made her remember other fires before she was born. She turned and an older woman inside her looked hard at me.

"My grandmother's family were from Leipzig. They had a famous apple garden. Who are you, the Devil?"

"Don't be shocked. It is the way it happens."

"How?"

"Touch of the poet. It has almost killed me. Fatal radiation. Do you want more photographs?"

"No!"

Somewhere along the cultural fault-lines, objective fact had been invented, if only to limit this avalanche. As control, Fact managed the story technology and edited the scripts. It was not so good at the sub-texts, because the operation was never perfect. Bits of rejected stories escaped to breed their own nets of shadow-stories. They made pirate raids on over-edited accounts of both the world and experience until the lives of creations and creators were intertwined.

Perhaps the world was not a tale told by an idiot. Perhaps it was the inspired creation of some covered-wagon horse-doctor at the end of a long day.

Where could Deborah Rumford go now? Japan, Israel, where they still had something to live and fight for, and they worshipped brains as fire sent from heaven.

If she stayed, the Flatlanders would take her down with them. She'd be another Viewer, growing fat and brainless, drunk and drugged, falling off a Viewing settee, choking on her own brainless spew.

Meantime her project was going out of her control. Events, the powers that be, money, international corporate interests were swamping her. Science was never really happy with unique individuals. They could hardly be systemised. This meant that she could be vapourised overnight. No wonder she looked terrified. The certainty was that she had not spoken or related to an ordinary battered piece of low life like me for years. Everything had in the beginning been glittering, spectacular; now here was the fall.

"It's going out of your control."

"I'm being bought out."

"You're in more danger than that."

"There's nothing I can do."

"Keep in touch."

"Yes. For sure."

Biting her lip, she disappeared quickly behind a shuffling line of the last few somewhat baffled and ragged Rogues, amongst whom I recognised Peter, who was in handcuffs, and the tall blonde girl, who looked as if she had been badly beaten.

Sinister-looking individuals supervised the operation. They gave orders to men who carried boxes and drove forklift trucks carrying equipment.

The last thing I remember was Dr. Deborah's sad and exhausted Los Alamos face, terrified at what she had unleashed, but angry that it was now being taken from her.

And thus the Flatlanders had got rid of the Rumford Rogues. The project was too big, too complex, too exotic, and far too brilliant for the Flatlands. They had created the Industrial Revolution, and Shakespeare, but they hated their own native genius. The hardware (and in this case the wetware and the software) was shipping out to Japan, Israel and America, where both the money and the interest was. She did not want to live in any of these places, she said rather sadly. She said she liked England, even if it was like living in Finland with a bag over your head. Since there was no way she could get any kind of money from any antiquated Flatlands science foundations, she said she would become once again an isolated academic, hobbled, half-starved, and confined to theoretical papers which would never be peer-reviewed by any Flatland science faculty.

I saw Brentford Garage University for the last time as I was escorted from *Biggs House* behind a screen of guns and armour. Behind me I left bomb scares, fires and sirens. A screaming high wind that locals had not before experienced pushed grey smoke seared with blood red streaks over the entire area as the *muezzin* roared over the campus.

As for myself, the media and the great wide world forgot me as quickly as they had found me. As the smell of fresh-cut Christmas trees came from a passing lorry headed for the Portobello Road, the visits of both Betty and Svetlana were getting few and far between.

I was grateful for the *Manang* for company, I needed rest and recuperation. I tried to sort out countless letters of praise and condemnation from all over the world, but the thrill was gone, and I settled down for an end-of-year re-read of Shakespeare, James Joyce, and Joseph Conrad.

epilogue

Two Late Arrivals

CHRISTMAS EVE in the Tabernacle. The Pethers clan invited me to a party, but I was not in the mood. I came back into my room, where the *Manang* was cooking one of her famous fish curry pies for the *zec* Christmas dinner on the morrow. This famous pie was two feet in diameter, and cooked in a huge fat wok on four gas burners. In the deep *Tabernacle* past, its kind had blown off the hats of many a junky, speed-freak, nose-sucker, and captive maniac yearning for deconstruction.

It must have been the aroma of a thousand years that inspired me to try and resume my neglected reading.

After a thimble of *Tree Frog*, I settled down to read and take further notes on Joyce's short story, *Araby*. I had compiled some thoughts and observations with a view to writing an article on this story to be published in *The Brentford Sceptic*. The paper had gone upmarket due to my adventures, and the lawnmower sales and Shared Green House Schemes had gone with the Flatland wind. Price was now smoking cigars and offering a variety of what he called "fine wines" from *Asda* to visitors, though his pronunciation of the names on the labels had to be heard to be believed.

I had just written of the last scene of *Araby*:

> *Night has fallen. A universe of lights, love, and inspiration is being taken apart before the boy's eyes. There is nothing but the hard road ahead and cruelty of new growth. Forever the boy will recall the railings and the lamppost of the twilight street, the braided hair of Mangan's sister, and the blinding pain of a dying evening which quickly vanished*

both his vision of the girl and the infinite magic of the very last hours of
his youth.
This image will last unto death. Perhaps he will see Mangan's sister
standing there when his soul takes its last flight…

I could not complete the sentence because somewhere in the high
dome of the Tabernacle a great clapper bell sounded. Freddy the module cat, quite astonished, left onto my open volume of Aristotle's *Poetics*
like a jet-propelled bath-bun, for all the world as if he was protecting
the work from some Satanic visitation.

It was later said that no-one had rung this bell since Great Victoria
died. Thinking I might meet the battlement ghost of General Gordon
or Disraeli, with my Browning in my hand I looked through stained
glass onto the forecourt and saw an astonishing sight.

Below my first floor window, covered in snow, stood Deborah Rumford with a shivering Rogue Thelma at her side, no less.

And both with suitcases.

Rogue Thelma, wearing a wig and dark glasses, and carrying a small
box wrapped in Christmas paper, At her side in a long black cloak,
stood Deborah, Though she still had something of her old grandeur,
she looked somewhat abandoned and forlorn. She became in the darkening evening a fugitive shadow standing on one of those wartime train
platforms that had proved such a horror to her race.

Two sighing voices on the Christmas wind:

"Help us!"

Telling the *Manang* to put the kettle on, I ran downstairs to let them
in, my mother's famous last words echoing in my head:

Don't laugh tae much. Laughter won't get ye through the winter!

I was not laughing at all at the thought that I would have to do a lot
of explaining to Warden Sproat upon the morrow.

finis

about the author

AFTER LEAVING Hallcroft School at the age of eighteen, in the course of what he calls "a delightfully misspent youth," Colin Bennett was employed as a musician (tenor sax) and later as a mercenary soldier. He says he was far better at the second than the first. Subsequently he read English at Balliol College, Oxford, and afterwards wrote the novels *Infantryman* (Fourth Estate) and *The Entertainment Bomb* (New Futurist Books). His next book was *Looking for Orthon* (Cosimo Books), a biography of George Adamski, the 1950s UFO visionary and first claimed "abductee". *Politics of the Imagination* (Headpress) followed. This is a biography of the American writer Charles Fort, who spent his life hunting down reports of "anomalous phenomena" or what he called "damned" events such as rains of frogs, cattle mutilations and UFO sightings. *Politics of the Imagination* was awarded Biography of the Year (2002) by Paraview Books, New York. John Nash, Nobel Prize winner, described it as "really very stimulating and the derived theme concept that the British may be too critical and resistant to imaginative concepts is also interesting."

Colin followed this book with *An American Demonology*, the story of the head of the 1950s United States Air Force UFO-hunting agency Project Blue Book.

He writes for *Nexus*, *Paranoia Magazine* and is a regular feature writer for (US) *UFO Magazine*. He is contributor to Nick Redfern's new book, *Contactees*.

185

A HEADPRESS Book
First published in 2009

HEADPRESS
Suite 306, The Colourworks
2a Abbot Street, London, E8 3DP, UK

Tel: 0845 330 1844
Email: headoffice@headpress.com
Web: www.headpress.com

THE RUMFORD ROGUES
Scenes from Consumer Life

Text copyright © Mr Colin Bennett
This volume copyright © 2009 Headpress
Design & layout: Mr David Kerekes & Mr Thomas Campbell
Proofing: Ms Philomena & Ms Jennifer Wallis
Headpress diaspora: Mr Caleb Selah,
Mr David, Ms Shelly Lang & Ms Bianca

British Library Cataloguing in Publication Data
A catalogue record for this book is available
from the British Library

ISBN 9781900486750

www.headpress.com